Praise for Wendy Dalrymple

"Cursed objects, an ancient cult, and a folklore thread that reminded me of *Sleepy Hollow*, Dalrymple's *Credenza* builds to a startling climax as it untangles the roots of the past. A genre blend that feels both modern and ancient."

Catherine McCarthy, author of *Mosaic* and *The House at the End of Lacelean Street*

"A deliciously horrific tale about a haunted heirloom with a life all its own. Brimming with sinister family secrets and twists galore, *Credenza* will have vintage lovers eyeing their collections with a newfound wariness. Dalrymple's wry, darkly humorous voice firmly establishes her as the queen of contemporary pink horror. You'll devour this book in one bite!"

Paulette Kennedy, bestselling author of *The Devil and Mrs. Davenport*

CREDENZA

CREDENZA

WENDY DALRYMPLE

Credenza
written by Wendy Dalrymple
published by Quill & Crow Publishing House

Library of Congress Control Number: 2025907176

Printed in the United States of America

Cover Design by Fay Lane

Edited by Cassandra L. Thompson

ISBN: 978-1-958228-86-9

ISBN: 978-1-958228-85-2 (ebook)

Publisher's Website: quillandcrowpublishinghouse.com

To all the mothers and daughters.

Prologue

"CUT IT DOWN."

The wind whipped at Peter's back in sharp, cruel gusts that cut through his threadbare coat straight to the bone. The ax handle was heavy in his hands as he stared at the stranger with uncertainty under a moonless night sky. Overhead, the naked branches of the twisted old walnut tree shivered in the breeze.

"The old Burgemeester tree?" Peter asked. "But, sir. The old mothers in town… They say not to—"

"Do as I tell you, boy!"

The back of the man's hand met the side of Peter's face with a shocking sting.

Peter gasped but was too afraid to say anything more. At dusk, the man in the scarlet cloak had plucked him from his nearby farm while splitting wood. The man had an accent Peter did not recognize and dark, refined features that seemed out of place for his village. Though his first instinct had been to run, he listened to the man's unusual task. It had been an unusually cruel winter for the family, and Peter couldn't say no to the promise of silver, even from a stranger.

"Do it now!"

The unearthly tone in the man's voice caused the milk Peter had consumed at dinner to curdle in his guts. Trembling with weak knees and a bruised cheek, Peter wished he had listened to his instincts.

He pushed past his fear, gripped the ax handle, and swung. He knew the consequences of cutting down the tree—of disturbing the resting place of the most wicked of men. He had spent many a dark night as a child at his grandmother's feet, listening to her tales of warning and woe by the fire. Still, with the menacing man at his back and the promise of a much-needed payment clawing at his mind, Peter felt he had no other choice. He gritted his teeth and swung.

The ax blade planted into the trunk of the tree with more difficulty than he expected. One chop. Two chops. Three. Peter was skilled when it came to felling trees, but walnut was a particularly hardy wood. He was cold and frightened, but as he plunged his blade into the trunk for the fourth time, his fear crystallized into pure terror. A gush of red spilled forth from the wound Peter had created with his ax. Bright and steaming, the crimson fluid splashed out onto the snow, filling Peter's nostrils with the metallic tang of blood. He gasped again and jumped back as it splashed his boots.

"Why have you stopped?" The stranger shoved at his back. "Keep cutting!"

His heart froze as Peter willed his petrified body to move. He brought the ax back and urged his body to move again lest he not meet the full wrath of this stranger.

Chop. Chop. Chop.

With each swing, hot arcs of red splashed Peter's face and breeches, turning the freshly fallen snow around him into a slurry of crimson slush.

Chop. Chop. Chop.

After what seemed like an eternity, with the muscles in his arms and back aflame, Peter swung his ax for the last time. The ancient walnut tree released a final torrent of blood and let out a roar through the frozen valley as it tumbled to the ground with an earth-shattering boom. Panting, Peter turned to the man with his hand outstretched.

"There. I've done it," he said. "Now pay me, and I'll be on my way."

The stranger swung a swift, sharp jab into the soft center of his belly. Peter winced as something hot and sticky pooled onto the front of his tunic. He brought a hand to his stomach and touched the place where the stranger had punched him, his vision blurring as he brought a palm up to his face. This time, his hands were awash in blood, this time his own. Before Peter lost consciousness, the stranger held a red-stained knife to his neck and slid the blade from one side of his throat all the way across.

"Here's your payment," the stranger hissed.

Chapter One

I WAS two years old the first time my grandmother's credenza drew blood. The story told to me was that I toddled into the dining room one afternoon while my mother was napping and stumbled over a lamp cord. My eyebrow connected with the sharp corner of the wooden cabinet and the origins of my distinctive scar became family lore. Even though the collision left a sizable gash, my grandmother said I didn't cry until I realized I was bleeding. Child safety measures weren't much of a thing yet in the 1980s, I suppose, and that wasn't the first or last time I would end up in harm's way. I cheated death often as a kid, even ending up at the bottom of a swimming pool at one point. It's a miracle that I made it to adulthood at all.

I always knew that the credenza was destined to be mine someday. When Grandma Maddie passed away the week after my 35th birthday, I got the call from her caregivers to come pick it up. The credenza was an outdated piece of furniture no one else in the family wanted anyway, a mid-century monster with a vintage aesthetic, pleasing only to those who enjoy kitsch, like myself. Most of my grandmother's belongings had been scattered to the winds over a decade ago when she was admitted to Heron's Bay Assisted Living Facility. My uncles got rid of most of her things before selling the house my grandfather built to a nice family from New Jersey. They didn't get the credenza, though. Before her memory loss advanced, Grandma Maddie had insisted the vintage cabinet should stay with her, no matter what.

And so, I found myself on a sweltering Florida afternoon in August, standing outside Heron's Bay with my daughter, Star, ready to collect my grandmother's favorite piece of furniture. I didn't know if Star and I could move the heavy credenza on our own, but I couldn't afford movers, and I certainly didn't want to leave it at the facility to be trashed. We had a dolly and a rented moving truck, and that would have to be good enough.

Star was a good kid. Even though Grandma Maddie's memory continued to decline after she was admitted, my daughter still found a way to bond with her. She came with me to every visit so we could paint my grandmother's nails, do her hair, and watch reruns of *Golden Girls* and *Seinfeld*. Visits had always been bittersweet, but now the fact that I would never see her again sat in my gut like a stone. As I reached for the front door handle to the white and pink building that afternoon, a wave of sorrow and regret crashed into my chest.

"You okay?" Star placed a hand on my shoulder.

I turned to face her and wiped at my cheek. "I just feel so…guilty."

"Because of Gran?"

I nodded and sucked in a lungful of humid air. "I hate that she wasn't home with us. I hate that she spent so many years here."

"I was a baby when she got sick," Star said. "There's no way you could have taken care of us both on your own."

"I know, I know. It just hurts. I'll never see her again, and this was the last place she was at and…oh, fuck." Another wave of grief knitted my throat closed. I swallowed the pain down. "Sorry. Let's just get this thing in the truck and get it home."

I opened the door and was greeted with a blast of chilly, disinfectant-scented air. Heron's Bay was just like many other assisted living facilities in Southwest Florida: clean, quiet as a tomb, and vaguely tropical-themed. My uncles didn't do a whole lot for their mother and didn't visit often, but they at least had the forethought to place her in a center that focused on memory care. Over the last decade of visits, Star and I had gotten to know the staff there fairly well. They had all been so good to my grandmother, a fact that I appreciated. It broke my heart that so many of the elderly folks there never got visitors, though, as one of the nurses pointed out, for some of them, there was probably a reason. In Grandma Maddie's case, I couldn't help but feel annoyed at my uncles for not visiting more.

I approached the front desk and managed a smile as I was greeted by Fernando. At nearly seven feet tall and with a build that could fill out a doorway, he looked more like a professional wrestler than a nurse. Fernando had been working at Heron's Bay almost as long as my grandmother had been a resident. He was always ready with a joke and a smile for Star and me.

"Hey, Ronnie," he said, coming out from behind the desk. "Good to see you."

"Good to see you, too."

Fernando gave me a friendly embrace, the scent of his spicy cologne stinging my nose. "I had some of the orderlies move the cabinet and a box of Miss Maddie's things into the hallway for you," he said. "I'm glad you came today because they were going to have to throw it all out tomorrow."

"Thanks for letting me know," I said. "That cabinet is a beast."

"You need any help moving it?"

"No. I appreciate the offer, though," I said. "I don't want you to get in trouble for leaving the front desk. Star and I can handle it."

"Yo." Fernando smiled, holding his hand up in anticipation of a high-five. "How's your summer break been?"

"Today's the last day." Star jumped to meet his high-five with her palm. "I'm going into middle school tomorrow."

"Time flies so fast," Fernando said. "You were just a little thing when I first met you. I'm sad we won't see you here anymore."

"I've got your number. We'll hang out sometime," I said, knowing that probably wasn't true. I wasn't the best at keeping up with friends despite my good intentions.

Fernando nodded. "Okay, well, just yell if you need any help. You know where to find me."

"Thanks."

I steeled myself as we headed down the hallway toward my grandmother's old room. Star towed the dolly behind me, the wheels squeaking against the polished terrazzo flooring. My heart clenched as I walked the well-worn path, nodding at a couple of other long-time residents who sat outside their doors to pass the time. This was going to be the last time I ever walked down this hall, and the reason for me coming here in the first place was gone forever. Without Grandma Maddie, the space felt emptier. Endless.

I turned the corner, and the credenza came into view, the sharp edge that once put a dent in my eyebrow glaring at me from a distance. I stared at the glossy finish, the warm brown walnut mesmerizing me. Seeing the vintage furniture again caused my adrenaline to spike. The fluorescent overhead lighting flickered and hummed as I approached, and the fine hairs on the back of my neck bristled. There was so much baggage tied to it, this one final relic of my disbanded family. A single cardboard moving box sat atop the cabinet, the name "Marquette" in black permanent marker.

"There it is." I sighed and turned toward my daughter. "Let me see the dolly."

Star wheeled the cart toward me, her face scrunched. "How are we gonna get it on there?"

I pursed my lips and evaluated the situation. Star had a point. The credenza floated on four slim, tapered legs. It would be nearly impossible to scoot the cabinet onto a dolly in its natural standing position without one of the skinny legs breaking.

"We'll have to turn it on its side," I said, grabbing the cardboard box. "I'll take this end; you go on the other. We can lay it on its back first."

"Okay." Star shrugged and tucked a bleach-blonde and purple strand of hair behind her ear. "You know, we can ask Fernando to help."

"We will if we have to," I said. "I just want to try this first. Remember, lift with your knees, not your back."

"I know." Star sighed.

I ran my hand along the walnut top, finding the finish dusty but still in excellent condition. Even though my grandmother's cabinet had lived through three children, an accident-prone granddaughter, and a move to the residential center, the wood appeared to be mostly free of nicks, scrapes, or discoloration. I placed one hand underneath the cabinet and one along the back and met Star's gaze.

"Ready?"

She nodded. "Yep."

"All together now," I said. "One, two, three."

I strained, my back twinging as we moved the cabinet away from the wall and slowly began to lean it back. Laying it down on the ground proved easy enough, but now we had to position it vertically so we could wheel it out the door. I moved to Star's side to push the heavy piece up together.

"Okay, steady," I said.

I slid my hand along the back of the cabinet, and a searing pain ripped through my finger. "Ow, fuck!"

I tugged my hand away from the cabinet, and a pinprick of bright red blood surfaced on the pad of my left pointer finger. I clenched my hand to my chest protectively, studying the wound. A sliver of wood was buried deep under the skin. I stuck the finger in my mouth and sucked, my tongue hit with the old-penny taste of iron.

"What happened?" Star asked.

"Splinter." I shook my hand, the fingertip throbbing as I examined the wound. "Dammit. It's deep, too."

"Want me to help get it out?"

"No," I said. "Let's just get this thing on the dolly. I'll take care of it at home."

"Okay."

"Just like before, on three."

My back muscles spasmed as Star helped me to lift the cabinet to a vertical position. We struggled a little but managed to scoot the cabinet onto the dolly. Star grabbed the cardboard box, and I tilted the cabinet back and we began the precarious journey of wheeling the considerable piece of furniture out to the car.

Fernando met us at the entrance and held the door open as we eased the credenza out of the building. There was a moment going down the ramp where I cursed myself for not bringing straps to tie the cabinet down, but by some miracle, we reached the rental truck without incident. Star helped me unload the credenza onto an old comforter, and the job was done. I stashed the cardboard box in the back of the truck, closed the door, and winced as the splinter throbbed under my skin.

I slid behind the wheel, stuck the key in the ignition, and turned the engine over. Star climbed into the passenger seat, and as she buckled her seatbelt, I got a sudden wave of nostalgia, reminded that she wasn't a little kid anymore. A premeditated feeling of loss threatened to close up my throat again as her life fast-forwarded before my eyes. My thoughts flashed back to her first time sitting in the front seat, coming home from her first day of third grade with chubby, flushed cheeks and a gap-toothed grin. The days were flying by too fast —*she* was growing up too fast. The combination of losing my beloved grandmother and the realization that my daughter was growing up hit me in the chest like a closed fist. I wiped at the wetness in my eyes and glanced up at the building towards the room where my grandmother had lived for ten years. I blinked as I tried to make sense of what I was seeing.

A figure was standing in the window. An elderly woman with a puff of snowy hair. She was staring at me. Watching me. *Grandma Maddie?*

"Mom?"

I gasped and brought a hand to my chest as I turned to face Star. Her lips were pursed, her eyes narrowed into a doubtful expression. I was acting like a "weird mom" again. I looked back at the window. Whoever had been standing there was gone.

"Sorry. I thought I saw something," I said, forcing a smile. "Wanna pick up some lunch on the way home?"

"YES. I'm STARVING," Star said, rolling her eyes. A teenager in training.

I threw the engine into reverse and backed out of the assisted living home on autopilot. I clenched the steering wheel, and a shock of pain zapped at my finger, reminding me of the splinter stuck in my skin. We bumped along down US-41 toward home in silence, my stomach growling in need of lunch, too.

In the back of the rental truck, the drawers of the credenza rattled.

Chapter Two

VERONICA

BLINDING sunlight assaulted my eyes as we drove the credenza away from Herons Glen in the rented delivery truck. I cursed myself for leaving my sunglasses at home, wincing against the harsh rays of light. The main road home, US-41, was a palm tree-lined sprawl of concrete strip malls, fast food chains, and gas stations, a stark contrast to the few original buildings from the 1960s that made up my neighborhood. We sped past the abandoned Tropic Isles Baptist Church where I used to attend Girlscout meetings, the scent of the moldy orange carpet and dusty wooden hues still fresh in my memory. The rusted-out warehouse that used to be the only roller skating rink in town loomed darkly next to the church, vines creeping up over the face of the cartoon mascot on the Palace Roller Rink sign. It hurt my heart to know that Star wouldn't be able to zip around those wooden floors on eight wheels to escape the heat like I did at her age, laughing with her friends as pop music blasted over crackling speakers.

Finally, we reached our neighborhood, and I braked at the main intersection, my thoughts lost to a time before, and my gaze trailed to finger-like palm tree frond shadows as they danced along the sizzling pavement. In the distance, heat waves shimmered against the blacktop, mesmerizing me while a blast of blissfully cool air conditioning kissed my heated cheeks and sweaty brow. Afternoon drives in South Florida were daze-inducing and exhausting, especially in the dead of summer when temperatures neared triple digits. The suburban commute wrapped my already grief-weary mind in a wet, woolen blanket of hypnotic tedium. I could have remained lost in my daydream of happier times when I was a kid, zipping around these familiar streets with friends. I felt safer then. More like myself.

Honk.

My shoulders jumped as the tropical suburban landscape came back into focus.

"Mom," Star said. "The light's green."

"Sorry."

I snapped out of my haze and hit the gas. Home was a 900-square-foot bungalow built in 1967 with two bedrooms, one bath, and a sunroom that doubled as my workspace and storage area for my shop. It was tiny, but it was all that Star and I needed, and it was mine. I had spent the last decade slowly renovating the place and returning it to its mid-century glory, from the starburst light fixtures right down to the retro appliances in the kitchen. Creating a vintage aesthetic in my home was a tedious and sometimes expensive obsession, but as an online antique and vintage goods retailer, it was also my business.

"Where is this thing gonna go?" Star asked, holding the door open as I wheeled the credenza up the walkway.

I winced, hoping the makeshift ramp I fashioned out of an old piece of pressboard would hold the weight of the cabinet. "Next to the kitchen table. It's supposed to be part of a dining room set, but we'll have to make do."

I used all my strength to wheel the cabinet through the entrance, trying my hardest not to bang the sharp corners against the door frame. Star helped me ease the credenza off the dolly, and together, we pushed our small dining table out of the way to make room. The walls of my kitchen were painted in robins' egg blue, illuminated by the white reclaimed saucer bubble pendant lamps I had found in an Orlando trade show. I had only finished redecorating a week before and still hadn't moved the furniture back. The timing couldn't have been more perfect to bring the credenza home.

We centered the long, rectangular cabinet on the wall opposite the window as sweat stung my eyes. More than fifty years of dust and family memories resided in its cracks and grooves, along with who knows what kind of germs from the assisted living center. A deep cleaning would be in order, but I wanted to get the heavy piece of furniture positioned first.

"Phew, that was quite a job." I wiped my brow, my

throbbing finger reminding me I had a splinter to remove. "Thank you for helping me."

"Can I go to Kayla's now?" Star's gaze darted toward the front door.

"Yeah, just bring in the box from the back of the truck for me first. I have to go get this splinter out," I said.

"Where do you want me to put it?"

"On top of the cabinet is fine."

"Okay."

Star made a beeline for the truck as I entered the bathroom. The large soda I had gulped down on the ride home sloshed in my stomach, the taste of fast food fries queasy on my lips as I pondered the task at hand. I opened the medicine cabinet and located the tweezers and some rubbing alcohol to begin my DIY surgery. The splinter was lodged into the forefinger on my dominant hand, so removing it would be tricky. I splashed alcohol on the red bump on the pad of my finger and assessed the situation. I couldn't see the splinter, but I tried to pinch at it with the tweezers just the same. Nothing.

The front door slammed as I heard Star return with the box. I reached for one of my disposable razors and contemplated my next move as she shouted through the house.

"Heading over to Kayla's!"

"Have fun! Love you!" I called out, gripping the razor between my middle finger and thumb.

I splashed the razor with rubbing alcohol.

The front door slammed again.

I let out a long, slow breath and positioned the blade over the wound.

With a small incision, a trickle of red oozed out from the splinter entrance. I placed the razor on the bathroom sink and squeezed my throbbing finger. Success. A little brown pinprick emerged from deep within the fleshy pad. I grasped the tweezers again and plucked at the bloody end of my finger until I was able to get hold of the splinter. I pulled it out and felt instant relief.

"Got you, fucker," I chuckled to myself, triumphant.

I wiped the splinter on a piece of toilet paper and splashed my finger again with rubbing alcohol for good measure. The wound still bled a little, so I applied antibiotic cream and wrapped my finger in a bandage. I caught sight of the scar on my eyebrow, feeling it pulse in time with my wounded finger. Grandma Maddie's credenza strikes again.

The house was quiet as I made my way back out to the open-concept living room and kitchen area. The silence made me uneasy, but I was slowly getting used to Star not being around as much and having more independence. It has been just the two of us for so long, and with no one else to help raise her, we were always together. I flipped the television on and let the laugh track of a sitcom fill the emptiness of my home and heart as I turned my attention to the cardboard box.

It was awful to think that my grandmother's memory was now reduced to a vintage piece of furniture and a single cardboard box of random things. My cheeks heated as I reached for the box, and my old friend Anger blossomed in my chest. Once again, I was doing a hard thing alone. I should have gotten used to it, but I was still bitter. I couldn't help but feel resentment for my absent partner, my absent extended family, and especially my own mother, who had disappeared before I reached kindergarten. Grandma Maddie had been the only person I could count on. I didn't want to leave that same legacy for my own daughter.

I ripped the clear shipping tape off the top of the box and readied myself for what was inside. Immediately, my heart broke as I reached into the treasure trove of items. On top of the pile was a pair of my grandmother's favorite pink and lace satin pajamas, still heavy with the flowery chemical cleaner scent I associated with the assisted living center. I smiled through a fresh crop of tears and sent up a silent word of thanks to Fernando for rescuing her things. My uncles had instructed Heron's Bay to donate all of her clothes and personal items, so he must have set these aside for me.

I placed the pair of pajamas on top of the credenza and reached inside the box again. I recognized the next item right away: a photo album I gave Grandma Maddie when she first entered the home. I had filled it with photos for her through the years, pictures of her children and Star, of her old friends and pets, and things she used to love. Although her memory was long gone, it made me feel good to show her all the wonderful things from her life. It felt good to share it with Star as well. It was to be our photo album now.

The rest of the items in the box must have been

random items from inside the credenza: an old cloth napkin, a plastic vase with fake flowers, a doily, a holiday print table runner, and an old book. But it was the item wrapped in newspaper at the very bottom of the box that piqued my interest.

The newspaper was old and yellowed, and a quick assessment told me it had been printed well before I was born. The vintage collector in me lit up with anticipation as I carefully unwrapped the heavy, strangely shaped object. My uncles must have missed this item when they were liquidating her home. A silver candlestick, perhaps? A vintage serving piece? It could have been anything.

My fingers closed around a textured, weighty handle, and the newspaper fell away to reveal a dangerous-looking blade. My eyes grew wide at the glint of sharpened metal attached to a curved handle that resembled the horn of some animal. I recoiled as I turned the knife over in my hand, both impressed and terrified at the shape and size of it. What on Earth could my grandmother have wanted such an ugly thing for?

I wrapped the knife back in the newsprint and stashed it back in the box. There were still a few more things to go through, but I didn't have it in me to deal with it at the moment. Moving the cabinet had proved to be more physically and emotionally taxing than I could have imagined, and I was drowsy thanks to my fast food lunch. I eased onto the couch as the last bit of energy melted away from my body. I stared at the television in an adrenaline-drained haze as the artificial sound of canned laughter lulled me into an afternoon nap.

———

"Veronica, help me set the table."

Grandma Maddie's voice floats out of the kitchen over the roar of football on the living room TV. It is Thanksgiving, and I am once again the only person helping my grandmother prepare our family meal.

I tightened the scrunchie on top of my head and opened the side door of the credenza. Grandma Maddie keeps all of her special occasion tableware in the dining room cabinet, and every Easter, Thanksgiving, and Christmas, it was my job to dig out the saucers and serving trays and dust them off.

I frown at Uncle Mike and Uncle James on Grandma's couch with their feet up, a half-dozen empty beer cans on the coffee table in front of them. I didn't know why Grandma Maddie tolerated their bad behavior and lack of help, but I could guess. Grandpa Eddie had died a long time ago, leaving her to raise my mother and uncles on her own. That, combined with my mom running off when I was little, made her want to hold on to whatever family was left. It was just easier to take their disrespect and mistreatment than to be alone.

I finish setting the table and wander into the kitchen, led by the smell of sage and thyme and roasting meat. I know I am dreaming, but I do not want to wake up. I am thirteen again, almost the same age as Star. I am cloaked in the warm familiarity of my grandmother's cooking and home. I am safe and loved. I am home. My chest aches as Grandma Maddie's back comes into view, standing at the kitchen counter and peeling potatoes in her housecoat and slippers. I missed her terribly.

"Veronica, there you are," she says, turning to me with a smile. Her cloud of white permed hair glows golden in the overhead light. "Would you check the oven for me?"

"Sure, Gran."

I turn toward the oven and grasp the door handle.

"We mustn't let it dry out," she says.

I open the oven door and peer inside to see what is cooking. It isn't a ham or a turkey or a tray of green bean casserole. It's something that makes no sense at all.

Roasting in the middle of my grandmother's oven is none other than a human head.

Chapter Three

VERONICA

"Mom. Wake up."

My eyes fluttered open as my chest exploded into a thousand panicked heartbeats. Star hovered over me with an expression of concern, her hand on my shoulder. The room was dark and the light outside our front picture window indicated that it was much later in the day than I would have liked. Dizzy, I sat up and tried to shake off the horrific scene from my dream. Charred skin. Gelatinous eyes melted into deep skull sockets. The scent of burnt hair even lingered in the back of my nostrils. I know my grandmother didn't actually bake a human head like it was a honey-glazed ham, but in the fleeting moments after waking, the dream felt very, very real.

"Sorry. I didn't mean to sleep so long," I rubbed my eyes. "I'll get dinner started soon."

"It's okay. I already ate tacos at Kayla's." Star crossed her arms at her chest. "You were talking in your sleep."

"I was?"

"Mhmm."

"What was I saying?" I stood up and stretched.

"You were just saying 'no' over and over," she said. "You were kind of crying."

I nodded. "It's been an emotional day for me."

"Are you okay?"

"Yeah, I'll be fine." I forced a smile. "Do you have everything you need for school tomorrow?"

"I think so." Star reached into the back pocket of her jeans and pulled out her phone. "I got a text from Dad."

I froze. Eric. My forced smile melted away. "Oh?"

"He wants to pick me up after school tomorrow," she said. "He's got a job in town."

I cleared my throat as adrenaline continued to pump down my arms and legs. "Do you want to see him?"

Star shrugged. "Yeah."

"Okay then. Just text me, you know. Keep me updated." I sucked in a shuddered breath.

"Thank you." Star swooped in for a hug.

I relaxed a little and kissed the top of her head. "You're welcome."

"I'm gonna go take a shower."

"Okay."

Star released herself from my grip and headed toward the bathroom. I shook my head, walked toward the kitchen, and opened the refrigerator door, even though I wasn't hungry. Eric. Fuck. I knew this day was coming, but did it have to be on the first day of middle school?

I grabbed lettuce, tomato, and sliced turkey from the fridge, my head pounding as I began to assemble my dinner. Eric had been absent for most of Star's life, off chasing his own demons and unable to be a parent. We had only been dating for six months when I got pregnant, and by the time Star came around, our relationship was already rocky. He was sliding into heavy drug use, something I discovered way too late. He got clean five years ago and, shortly after that, began to call Star and make regular child support payments. Eric still owed me a ton of back support and owed his daughter years of parenting, but I could see that he was trying. It was easier for me to remain bitter and give him the cold shoulder, but I could never keep Star from knowing her family. Someday, I would be gone, and Star would need all the support and love she deserved. If she wanted to see her father, I wasn't going to stand in the way.

I cobbled a half-hearted turkey sandwich together through tears, and a dark chuckle escaped my throat. *When did I become such a big baby?* I grabbed my sad dinner, slumped back onto the couch, and stared at my sandwich. I knew it wasn't Star's job to keep me company, but with every passing year, I felt the ties that bonded us shift and change. I had no friends, no family, no life outside of being a mother and my work. If I didn't figure myself out, I was going to be a wreck when Star went off to college.

I put on a good face when Star returned from the shower in a mist of strawberry-scented body wash. We talked about middle school, about which friends she wanted to see, and what classes she was signed up for. She laid out her outfit for the following day and made her lunch before heading to bed.

I stayed awake on the couch that night, unable to fall back to sleep thanks to my late afternoon nap. Dread sat on my chest, sharp-clawed and heavy like a cat, ready to pounce. Something bad was on the horizon; I could feel it in my body. Only what that something was, I could not know.

———

"Have a great day, sweetie!"

Star grabbed her backpack and slid out of the passenger seat of my car the following morning. She smiled and waved back as she confidently navigated her way through a sea of pre-teens toward her new middle school. I watched as she disappeared through the front doors, my shoulders jumping as the car behind me blasted its horn.

"Fuck off." I swore under my breath and threw my car into drive. I didn't have all morning to sit around and be sentimental anyway. A half-dozen packages sat in the trunk of my car, ready to be dropped off at the post office and mailed off to clients. After that, I needed to return the moving truck to the rental place and figure out how I was going to get home. But before any of that, there was the estate sale down on McGregor Boulevard I needed to hit first.

Estate sales were my bread and butter when it came

to unearthing flippable vintage treasures. Grandma Maddie was the one who had turned me on to collecting and appraising vintage treasures. Going to yard sales, auctions, and swap meets was a favorite pastime of ours when I was a girl. Thrift stores used to be a good place to find unique collectibles, but in the last decade, more resellers than ever have jumped into the ring, severely limiting my potential stock. Still, I knew plenty of good stuff was hidden away in the closets of deceased, wealthy women.

Making connections with estate sale planners had proven to be a worthy investment. Linda was expecting me at the waterfront home near downtown Ft. Myers so I could get a fifteen-minute head start before the doors officially opened at 10 am. There was already a line of cars outside the home when I arrived, which I expected. Whenever there was an estate sale in this part of town, vintage furniture dealers and real estate looky-loos from across the state swarmed to get a peek. If not for my arrangement with Linda, I wouldn't be able to score half the fur coats, designer handbags, and collectible homewares I usually do.

With my wheeled hand cart and oversized sunglasses, I marched down the sidewalk on a mission. The hunt for Hermes scarves, vintage Coach bags, and art glass always got my blood pumping, the anticipation of what I might find fizzing through my body like electricity. Sometimes, I found items for my own home restoration purposes as well, but I tried to focus on collecting stock for my online boutique, Veronica's Vintage. I was so broke at the moment I couldn't even afford a used throw pillow if I wanted. Renting the truck to tow the credenza home had siphoned the last of my disposable income for the month.

I was nearly out of breath by the time I stomped up the long front walkway toward the imposing Mediterranean-style home. I held my head high as I breezed past the line of waiting hopefuls near the front door, each throwing pinched expressions at me like daggers. The usual murmur of disapproval followed me as Linda smiled and let me through the front door without comment. I paid her for this privilege, and I paid her well, but the people waiting outside the door didn't know that. I didn't care. This was my livelihood, and acquiring the items inside would help put food on the table for Star. They could all go to hell.

"Morning, Ronnie," Linda said, closing the door behind me. "Didn't think you were going to make it."

"Morning. I had to drop Star off. First day of middle school." I sighed and glanced up at the curved double staircase. This house wasn't just an estate. It was a mansion. "Is the master bedroom up that way?"

"Yes, to the right," Linda said, patting down her bob of short dark hair. "You're going to have a field day with that closet."

"Perfect. I'm off then." I folded up my hand cart, tucked it under my arm, and began my ascent up the staircase. The decor was all white marble and wide windows overlooking the navy blue expanse of the Caloosahatchee River. My thoughts always turned to the owners of the house whenever I began the process of rummaging through their things. What kind of life did they lead to afford them such luxuries? Were they good people? Did they inherit their wealth or earn it somehow?

The master bedroom was upstairs and to the right, just as Linda had said. A quick appraisal of the space told me this one wing of the estate alone was the size of my entire home. An enormous bed dominated the center of the bedroom, the tassel coverlet straight as a pin and perfectly fitted to the floating bed frame as though it had never even been slept in. To the left was the master bathroom, outfitted with a walk-in shower for six and a clawfoot bathtub. But it was the walk-in closet opposite the bathroom that caught my eye.

A crystal chandelier hung from its ceiling, illuminating cubicles of shoes, a wall of drawers, and multiple racks bursting with hangers. I would need more than fifteen minutes to properly go through everything, but at least this way, I would get a head start. By the time I heard the commotion of pounding feet upstairs and the murmur of voices, I managed to snag two fur coats, a Vivienne Westwood dress, three Louis Vuitton handbags, and an unopened bottle of Chanel No. 5. I was already over my budget, but I knew I could easily make four times the profit on these items alone in my store. Hell, the Vivienne Westwood dress alone would pay for my mortgage for the month. If I could find the right buyer, that is.

I coasted out of the master bedroom with my goods and made a beeline for Linda before I could pick up any more items. Self-control and market know-how had made it possible for me to stay in the vintage resale game all these years. I had to learn marketing, social media, and all the other things that come with running a business, but keeping within my budget had always been the biggest challenge. Sometimes it was no fun to be surrounded by shiny, pretty things only to never be able to keep any for myself.

I paid Linda her asking price of $280 (ouch) and left the estate sale riding on a buyer's high. The dress and coats would need to be cleaned and I would have to condition and refinish the leather on the purses, but otherwise, I had made out very well. I was so lost in thought organizing the refurbishing to-do list of my new finds that I didn't hear the man call to me as I reached my car.

"Veronica? Veronica Marquette?"

I blinked and whipped my head around toward the voice. A man of indeterminable age stood on the sidewalk behind me, smiling with a row of perfect teeth. Veneers. The hair at his temples was silver, but his skin was smooth, his jawline square as a cartoon superhero. He was dressed impeccably—almost too well. A lawyer? A politician? It was hard to tell.

"That's me."

"You'll have to excuse me. Linda told me you would be here this morning. I've been trying to get in contact with you." The man reached into his pocket and pulled out a small silver business card case. He flipped it open, pulled out a card, and handed it to me. "I'm Paul Dietzer. I was an old friend of your grandmother."

I frowned, took the business card from him, and glanced at it. The card indeed said Paul Dietzer. It also stated that he was a vintage furniture dealer.

"My grandmother never mentioned you," I said, flicking the business card with my thumb. "Why did you ask Linda about me?"

"I'm sorry. I know this must seem very strange." Paul laughed, the corners of his eyes crinkling. "You see, I understand you've acquired a very important piece of furniture after your grandmother passed. I would like to buy it from you."

Chapter Four

MADELINE, 1962

"It's a real beauty, isn't it? Came over all the way from Copenhagen. Finest Danish craftsmanship you'll find around these parts, that's for sure."

Madeline Marquette appraised the price tag of the wooden cabinet and raised her eyebrows. The salesman standing before her was young and eager, but she was no fool. She was also a grieving widow on a budget and couldn't resist trying to get a bargain. She flicked her wrist and checked the time; it was getting late and she was due back home to relieve the babysitter soon.

"It is a nice piece," she said. "But I can get a sideboard over at Price Cutters for half the cost."

"Oh, but you see, this isn't a sideboard; it's a *credenza*," the salesman said.

"What's the difference?" Madeline ran her fingertips along the smooth wooden surface, trying to mask her admiration. In truth, she had been eyeing this piece of furniture for months, even before Ernie had his accident. Something about this particular cabinet called to her, as though she had to have it. As though it was always destined to be hers. Now that she had some unexpected cash at hand, Madeline could finally decorate her little home the way she saw fit. But still. Everything could be negotiated.

"You see, ma'am, this particular piece of furniture, well, it's not just furniture—it's art!" The salesman opened up the top drawer of the cabinet and waved Madeline over. "See here? This seal shows the name of the artist and how many of this particular style was made. This credenza is one of only thirteen of its kind."

"Is that so?" Madeline nodded, still trying to hide her interest.

"Oh, and!" The man adjusted his necktie and threw her a smile. "It's crafted from hundred-year-old walnut. Very hard, durable, high-quality stuff. You have kids, Mrs...?"

"Marquette," Madeline said. "Yes, three in fact. A baby girl and two boys."

"Excellent. Well, you can rest assured that this kind of high quality furniture can take all the nicks and wear-and-tear little ones are known for. Plus, it's a piece you'll be sure to pass down some day. A family heirloom, if you will."

"You have a point there." Madeline stood back to appraise the piece one last time. "Do you provide free delivery and setup?"

The salesman's grin grew wider. "We sure do."

She nodded, already imagining how the new piece of furniture would look next to her dining room table.

"I'll take it."

Chapter Five

VERONICA

It was difficult to focus on much else after meeting Paul Dietzer. It isn't every day that a stranger seeks you out to purchase an old heirloom for $10,000. But that's exactly what happened, and the encounter left me reeling.

I told Dietzer I would think about his offer and drove away from the estate sale with my heart in my throat. I wanted to call someone and tell them about the wild thing that had just happened to me, but there was no one to tell. I squeezed the steering wheel all the way to the post office, sorting through my bewilderment. Ten grand for an old cabinet? Surely, it couldn't be worth that much.

By the time I got home, my hands ached from clenching the steering wheel so hard. I flexed my palms and inspected my bandaged finger, surprised to find an inflamed bump where my splinter had been. *Great.* A trip to the urgent care clinic was exactly what my bank account needed. I placed my new purchases on my desk and headed to the bathroom to clean the wound again, saying a silent prayer that I could take care of it myself. The site of the wound frothed and bubbled like a science experiment as I poured hydrogen peroxide over it.

"Please don't be infected," I whispered to whatever deity would listen. "I just need to get through this rough spot, and then I can afford a doctor bill, okay?"

I squeezed my fingertip, and my stomach lurched as a glob of milky gunk gushed forth. I applied more antibiotic ointment, and when I was satisfied with my bandaging job, I grabbed the keys to the moving truck. All I wanted to do at the moment was get to work refurbishing my finds, but if I didn't get the moving truck back before closing time, I would lose my deposit. Hurt fingers and research would have to wait.

I stashed my bike in the back of the moving truck and shielded my eyes as I glanced up at the clear blue sky. It was only two miles from my house to the truck rental place, but I wasn't looking forward to biking home along a busy road. August was brutally hot in Florida, but I couldn't justify spending money on the taxi ride, especially after my estate sale shopping spree. I resigned myself to the task at hand, figuring I could use the exercise anyway, and drove toward the truck rental place.

Thirty minutes later, I found myself pedaling down Pondella Road under the punishing midday sun, my shoulders and arms slick with sweat. I had only biked a few blocks, but I already felt like I was dying. Before Star was born and I didn't have a car, I biked everywhere, but that was fifteen years ago. I was out of shape. I was exhausted. I was getting honked at by a passing car.

My pulse picked up speed as a new model black Honda pulled into the gas station in front of me and honked again. The driver's side window rolled down, and a familiar voice wafted toward me over the din of traffic.

"You just don't know how to ask for help, do you?"

I let out a sigh of relief as I instantly recognized the driver. A freshly shaven Fernando smiled at me from behind the wheel, his massive biceps popping beneath a fitted white tee. I realized as blood rushed to my already heated cheeks, that I had never seen him out of his scrubs before.

"Fernando!" I laughed and wiped my brow. "Hi."

"Need a lift?"

"Oh, no. I'm good," I said, panting. "I was just biking home from the truck rental place."

"*Ronnie*. It's like, a hundred degrees." Fernando rolled his eyes. "Come on, let me take you home."

I grimaced. He was right. I would probably collapse from heat exhaustion if I continued. "Will my bike fit in your trunk?"

"Sure. I've got something to tie it down. No problem." Fernando got out and lifted my bike off the ground like it was nothing.

I slid into the passenger seat of his car and was met with a welcome blast of air conditioning as he secured the bike to the trunk hood with bungee cords. I took a moment to glance around the inside of Fernando's car as he worked—the interior was neat as a pin and smelled just like him, all cinnamon, clean laundry, and something else I couldn't quite put my finger on.

"Which way is home?" Fernando asked, sliding behind the wheel.

"Just a couple of miles down that way," I said. "Thanks again."

"No problem. You and Star get that big old cabinet into the house, okay?"

"Mhmm. You know, the weirdest thing happened to me this morning. I was at an estate sale picking up some new stock for my shop, and this man came out of nowhere and offered to buy it."

"Your grandma's cabinet?"

"Yeah," I said. "He claimed to be friends with her, but I call bullshit. Grandma didn't trust many men, and even so, she never had anyone come around who wasn't family. Not that I remember, anyway."

"My Grandma had a whole life that none of us kids knew about." Fernando chuckled. "After she passed, we learned she used to be a pin-up model in, like, the 1950s, I think? Anyway, you would be surprised at the secret lives that people lead."

"Yeah, that's true. I just don't know how this guy even found me. It feels weird."

"Well, are you going to sell it?"

"I don't know. That's the tough part. He said he would pay me ten grand for it."

"Ten?" Fernando exclaimed. "Thousand? For that old cabinet? No offense, but damn. I would take it."

"I know. And trust me, I could use the money. I think

it was made by some kinda famous furniture designer? I dunno. I need to do some research and find out. Still, it seems suspicious."

"I don't blame you for being cautious. There are a lot of weirdos out there." Fernando flashed me a silly smile. "Like me."

"Oh please, you're about one of the only people I trust anymore," I said. My hand shot out instinctively and patted his hand as it rested on the shift stick. My cheeks heated again as I pulled my hand back, and suddenly, I began to feel very silly and self-conscious, like a teenager on a first date. Thankfully, we were almost to my house.

"Um, take a left just up there. It's, uh, 764 July Lane."

"You got it."

I clasped my hands in my lap the rest of the way. Fernando parked in my driveway and pulled my bike from his trunk, and I felt foolish all over again as I struggled to meet his gaze.

"Thanks again for the ride. I probably would have melted into the pavement if you didn't show up."

"You know you can call me if you ever need anything, right?"

I bit my lip and nodded. "I know. I need to get better about asking for help, I guess."

"Everyone needs a little help sometimes. Even Superwoman."

"Yeah, it's true." I let out a snort laugh. "But I'm hardly Superwoman."

"Veronica, I saw a lot of residents come and go over the years. No one visited as regularly as you *and* with a kid on your hip." He nodded toward the house. "And look at this place? It looks great! You take care of your home and Star on your own. If that doesn't qualify as Superwoman, then I don't know what will."

"Now you're just sucking up to me," I shifted my weight and glanced at the ground. Taking compliments was never my strong suit. "Maybe there is one more thing you can help me with."

"What's that?"

"I'm a mediocre cook," I said. "Wanna come by and help me and Star make dinner? Say, Friday night?"

"Well, you're in luck because I'm an excellent cook." Fernando smiled. "Six, okay?"

"Perfect."

"It's a date then." Fernando jingled his keys and gave me another knee-melting grin. "See you Friday, Veronica."

I waved and watched him back out of the driveway as feel-good chemicals clouded my brain. Fernando? Really? I supposed since he was no longer a caretaker for my grandmother that it wouldn't be a conflict of interest, but up to that point, the idea of dating hadn't even crossed my mind. Not with Fernando. Not with anyone. Still, I needed to take my own advice and try to get out there more, make more friends and connections. Easier said than done.

I spent the rest of the afternoon sorting through my new inventory pieces, answering emails from buyers, and writing up a to-do list for refurbishing, photographing, and cataloging my finds. All the while, my thoughts kept trailing back to the credenza. I still needed to clean it, but I wanted to do some research on it first. When I was finished with my work for the day, I pulled out the top drawer of the cabinet and inspected the label inside. I never felt right snooping around inside before while my grandmother was alive, and with her gone, it didn't feel any different. It felt intrusive, somehow. Still, I searched through the inside of the cabinets until I located the medallion-shaped label on the inside of the drawer. It read:

L. Andersen, Copenhagen

L. Andersen. Never heard of them before, but if this piece was as rare as Dietzer said, that's not a surprise. Even though I was well-versed when it came to vintage designers, there were still plenty of furniture craftsmen and artisans I didn't know about from abroad. A quick internet search on my phone didn't bring up anything about them, or Dietzer, either, for that matter. Before I had a chance to dig deeper, Eric's red Jeep pulled into my driveway.

I closed the door and took a deep breath.

Eric and I had been working toward this moment for the last six months. I didn't know if I would ever feel fully confident enough to have Star in his care after everything that happened, but I also knew I had to let go at some point. He was working hard to be a better person, and Star was eager to get to know him. As I walked out to the front door, Star exited from the passenger side, all smiles and my stomach unclenched.

"Hey," I said. "How was your first day of school?"

"Fine." Star slung her backpack over her shoulder and waved at Eric. "Bye, Dad."

Star gave me a brief hug and ran inside as I approached the driver's side window. Like myself, Eric was nearing middle age, though the last decade had been harder on him than me. He looked closer to fifty than forty and sported a shaved head, his physique thinner than I remember. His eyes were clear, though, and his body seemed more relaxed. At ease.

"Hi," I said. "Did you two have a good time?"

"Yeah. Thanks for letting me have her." Eric gave me a weak smile. "You look good."

"So do you." I cleared my throat. "Thanks for bringing her home."

"I'd like to do this again. If that's okay," he said. "I'll be in town working on a contract job for the next month, so I can pick her up after school. Mom was also asking if we could have her over for Thanksgiving this year."

My gut clenched. Thanksgiving was still a while away, but the thought of sharing my daughter for a holiday brought up a wave of unexpected anxiety. "We'll see. Did you ask Star if she wanted to?"

"No. I wanted to check with you first," he said. "Anyway, think about it."

"I will. Take care. We'll be in touch."

"Hey."

I turned to face my ex. The drug addict. The man who left me heartbroken and parenting an infant alone. A man who had even more demons than me to deal with. "What?"

"Thanks again. I know I don't deserve this second chance, but I appreciate it."

I shook my head. "I'm not doing it for you. I'm doing it for Star."

Eric nodded. "Still. Thank you."

With that, he pulled out of the driveway and into the night.

Chapter Six

VERONICA

"Fernando is coming over on Friday."

Star dropped the head of lettuce she was chopping on the floor. She'd offered to help me make dinner that night, but like me, she wasn't exactly skilled in the kitchen. She picked up the bundle of romaine and stared at me with a skeptical frown.

"Fernando? From the nursing home?"

"Assisted living facility. And yes, *that* Fernando."

"For a date?"

"No. Yes. Maybe. I don't know." I pulled a store-bought rotisserie chicken from the fridge. "He gave me a ride home today after I dropped off the rental truck."

Star wiggled her eyebrows at me. "He's kinda cute…"

"I don't know if he's my type," I said. "I'm just trying something new. You know. Gettin' outta my comfort zone."

"Good." Star paused, took a breath, and then began again. "Dad wanted to come pick me up Friday and take me out for pizza."

"Oh?"

"I don't have to have dinner with Dad if you want me here," she said. "Or I could go if you want some privacy."

I rolled my eyes. "Whatever you want to do is fine. I was just letting you know."

"That's cool." Star rinsed off the head of lettuce and continued to make the salad. "Who's Paul Dietzer?"

"Hmm?"

"The card over on Gran's cabinet."

"Oh. He's some furniture dealer who wants to buy the cabinet," I said. "I was going to tell you about it. He met me at the estate sale today and offered to buy it. I don't know if I'm going to sell it to him, though."

"How much was he going to pay for it?"

I paused. There weren't many secrets between Star and me, so there was no use trying to keep information from her now. "Ten thousand dollars."

"What! You're going to sell it to him, right?"

"I dunno."

"*Mom.* Every month, you complain about how poor we are. Wouldn't you like a little bit of extra cash? You know, to make things easier?"

"Yeah, but it was your grandma's." I groaned. "Trust me, it's a tough decision. I don't want to give the cabinet up, but that deal is too good to let go."

Star and I continued to chat about school and her

friends as we assembled our chicken salads. We watched her favorite K-drama while we ate dinner and afterward, cleaned up the kitchen together. Star went to take a shower, and I was left with a glass of red wine in one hand and my dusting rag in the other. If I was going to sell this cabinet to Dietzer, I wanted it to look as good as possible.

I started at the top, using Murphy's Oil Soap to dust and clean the surface, making sure to rub along the grain lightly. My injured finger ached as I worked, so I popped an ibuprofen and poured another glass of Merlot, hoping the combo would be a good enough painkiller. By the time I was finished with the exterior, Star appeared from the shower to give me a kiss goodnight. I poured myself a third glass of wine and began on the side cupboards where my grandmother used to store her special occasion plates. I still had those plates in a box in my closet, one of the few items she had given me herself before everything went bad. I had hoped to store the plates in the credenza again someday. Now, I wasn't so sure.

When I was done detailing the side cabinets, I moved on to the three drawers in the center, where my grandmother had kept extra table linens, napkins, candlesticks, and other tableware. I cleaned out the first two drawers without a problem, but when I got to the third drawer, I noticed that something was different. The wood lining the bottom of the drawer was a slightly different shade than the other two.

Shit. It occurred to me that Dietzer might not pay me the full amount for the credenza if there was a slight imperfection on the piece. I poked along the sides to see if the liner could be replaced and was surprised when it easily came away. The drawer liner lifted to reveal a false bottom with a hidden compartment beneath.

"That's weird." I replaced the false bottom, closed the drawer, and stood back to admire my work. I felt a pang of regret as I regarded the cabinet; it had shined up nicely and I really did love how it looked in my dining room. I figured I could at least enjoy having it in my home until I decided whether or not to sell. I grabbed a piece of vintage glassware and a framed photo of Grandma Maddie and myself when I was five years old from my bookshelf and arranged them on top of the credenza.

"Sorry, Gran," I said, downing the rest of my wine. "I'm broke, so this old beast might have to go."

I glanced at the photo of my grandmother, my heart hurting, the image of her a comforting presence. My gaze turned to little me, toothless and messy-haired in some neon print fashion catastrophe. I caught my reflection in the glass, and the heart-warming moment melted away as I nearly jumped out of my skin.

No.

A voice broke through the silence as an icy puff of air blew at the nape of my neck. In the reflection of the picture frame glass, I clearly saw someone standing behind me. The weight in the room pressed at my back as I gripped my wine glass, ready to smash it in the face of whoever was behind me. I spun on my heels, ready to strike, but was met with nothing but thin air.

There were few places for an intruder to hide in my small home, but I wasn't going to take any chances. I lunged toward the kitchen counter and grabbed a knife from the wooden block. My voice was shaky as I called out to whoever was in my home.

"You tripped my alarm! The cops are on their way!" I held the weapon out in front of me, feeling as helpless as Wendy in The Shining. "Leave now, and there won't be any trouble!"

I glanced at the front door and saw that the deadbolt was locked, as it always was when we were home. Whoever got in didn't come from there. The side door in my kitchen that led to the backyard was also locked. If there was an intruder in my house, then they either got in through a window or were already there and waiting when Star and I got home. I tiptoed down the hall to Star's room, where she was still awake, playing on her phone at her desk.

"Sorry, I was just going to bed." Her eyes grew wide at the knife in my hand. "What's going on?"

"I think there might be someone in the house," I whispered. "Or maybe I'm just crazy. I don't know."

"Should I call 9-1-1?" Star whispered back.

"No. Actually, yes. Stay here and lock your door. I'm going to check the other rooms."

I walked past the bathroom in the hallway and flicked on the light. Thankfully, Star once again forgot to close the shower curtain. A quick glance showed me that the bathroom was clear. The only place left for someone to hide was my bedroom.

I flicked on the light and swallowed, trying my best to sound bigger and braver than I really was. "Last chance, asshole. The cops are on their way. You should leave now."

Was I really going to check my closet for an intruder? Before I could make my heart beat any faster, I was interrupted by a bang and the sound of breaking glass. I sprinted on adrenaline-fueled legs down the hall toward the sound.

The photo of my grandmother and I had been knocked to the floor.

But no one was there.

———

"And you said that a picture frame was knocked over?" Officer Kincaid stood in my hallway as I hugged Star to my chest. The flashing lights of the ambulance in front of my house receded as it pulled away, its services no longer needed. Officer Kincaid stayed behind with her notebook in hand and a tired expression on her face.

"Yes. All of my doors and windows were locked, so I don't know how they got in here. Or how they got out."

"Mrs. Marquette, do you, by chance, have a cat or something?"

"It's Miss. And no, we don't have any pets."

Officer Kincaid sighed. "Well, nothing was taken from the house, and there's no sign of forced entry, so there's not much we can do. You might want to think about getting a security camera installed, though."

The police officer handed me her business card with a set of numbers printed on it. "This is my direct line and your case number. If you see or hear anything else or have any other information, just call."

"Thanks." I took the business card, feeling very defeated and foolish, as I let the police officer out and locked the front door. Maybe she was right. A video security system didn't sound so bad. Paying for it, on the other hand, would be a problem.

"Can I sleep with you tonight?" Star hugged her stuffed dog pillow to her chest, her purple highlights frizzing around her head like a violet halo. Even though she was getting older, my daughter was still a little girl in many ways.

"Yeah. I'm sorry I spooked you," I said. "It was probably my imagination. Don't worry. When I get my next payment from a client, I'll look into getting cameras or something."

"Okay."

"Go get into bed. I'll be right there."

I double-checked the back door and turned out the lights, exhausted but wide awake, thanks to our visit from the police. I glanced at the credenza again, where the picture was still lying face-down in a pile of glass. I hadn't wanted to touch it just in case the police wanted to do fingerprints or something. I picked up the frame and frowned at the crack in the glass. A jagged line ran all the way down the center across my grandmother's face.

I wasn't the type of person to see things or make up stories. I didn't believe in ghosts or the supernatural, but now, I wasn't so sure. Someone—or something—had been in my home. I was certain.

I stayed wide awake all that night, listening to every creak in my home, every click of the refrigerator, every sigh of the air conditioner. Waiting for something else to give me another sign. But that sign never came, and finally, my exhaustion got the best of me, and my body gave in to sleep.

Chapter Seven

KAREN, 1972

KAREN MARQUETTE WAS HOME ALONE when she heard a knock at the front door. Her mother had gone out for milk and eggs, and her two older brothers were riding bikes with their friends in the neighborhood. It was a bright and beautiful Saturday morning in fall, and all Karen wanted to do was hide inside and watch *Josie and the Pussycats*. Her gaze flicked from the rock 'n roll cartoon girls on the TV screen to the front door, and her heart leaped to her throat as another round of insistent knocks began. No one in the neighborhood locked their doors, and that morning, the Marquette family's front door was unlocked, too.

Bang, bang, bang.

Karen gasped and jumped off the couch, hurling her little body toward the console TV. She wound the knob to turn down the volume, but it was too late. Whoever was knocking knew that someone was home. She crouched low under the front picture window and made herself as small as possible under the curtains in an attempt to hide. A shadow passed in front of the slotted glass jalousie windows just over her head, and a stranger's muffled voice called out to her.

"I know you're in there, little girl," the stranger said. "I just need to ask you a question."

Karen held her breath and squeezed her knees to her chest. Maybe she could make herself invisible, and then the stranger would go away. Maybe her brothers would come home and scare the guy off. Maybe…

Her ears perked at the rumble of her mother's Pontiac pulling into the driveway. Relief spilled down her anxious little body as the stranger's shadow receded overhead. She turned and gripped the tiled windowsill to peek outside and saw a tall man in a dark suit approach her mother's car.

Karen strained to hear what the man was saying as her mother unloaded the groceries from her trunk. She couldn't make out any words, but from the expression on her mother's face, she could tell that the man was not welcome. The stranger gave her mother a small white business card and glanced back toward the house one last time before walking away. Karen's pulse was still pounding when her mother opened the front door.

"Mama!" She ran to her mother, burying her face into the skirt of her seersucker dress. "Who was that man?"

"I don't know," she said. "You didn't open the door for him, did you?"

Karen shook her head. "No, ma'am."

"Where are your brothers?"

"Riding bikes."

"They should be here with you. I'm going to tan their hides." Her mother sighed and handed her the paper grocery bags. "Put these away, will you?"

"Sure, Mama."

Karen took the bag of groceries and headed toward the kitchen. She unloaded the gallon of milk and placed it in their refrigerator, then stuck the loaf of bread in the bread box. When finished, she folded the paper bag and tucked it away in the linen closet. She returned to find her mother staring at the credenza in the living room with the business card in her hand. Her mother turned to face her with a strange sort of look, her lips pursed together in an expression of worry and confusion.

"What did that man want, Mama?"

Her mother shook her head. "He wanted to buy our credenza. I don't know how he even knew we owned it. You're sure you didn't let him into the house?"

Karen nodded emphatically. "I'm sure. I would never let a stranger into the house."

"Good," she said, crumpling the card into a ball. "If you ever see that man again, you tell me. Something about him gave me the willies."

Chapter Eight

VERONICA

STAR WOKE up bright-eyed and full of energy the following morning after our break-in scare, as though nothing had ever happened. I was fortunate to have such a resilient child, especially after the drama the night before. I was still a ball of nerves as I drove her to school, tired but jittery from the combination of too much coffee and a lifetime of unchecked anxiety. I worried I wouldn't be able to focus on my work, but when I returned home that morning, I was ready to dig into my shopkeeper duties.

I began by hand washing the Hermes scarves in Woolite and drying them flat on special racks. I was all out of leather conditioner, and the fur coats would have to be sent to a special cleaner. Fur coat sales did better closer to winter, so I would have to wait to list those for a while anyway. I answered some emails from potential clients about a pair of shoes and a vintage brooch in my shop and even sold a cocktail dress I had purchased last spring from an estate sale. By noon, I was ready for lunch, but a knock made me lose my appetite altogether.

I peered through the peephole, and all of the feeling left my arms and legs. The person on the other side of the door was just as terrifying to me as whoever might have been in my house the night before.

"I know you're there," my mother said, pressing her mouth to the crack in the front door. "I can see your shadow."

Instantly, my pulse began to slam in my neck. Karen Marquette was not welcome in my home. Not now. Not ever.

"What do you want?" I demanded.

"I hear you have mom's cabinet."

"So?"

"Look, I know you hate my guts. You have that right, but I just need you to listen to what I have to say."

"You're trespassing."

"Jesus, Veronica. This is serious!"

"*I'm* serious!" Tears sprung from the corners of my eyes. *What the hell was going on?*

"Weird stuff is happening, right?"

I blinked and leaned against the door, my hands balled into fists. How could she know? My injured finger pulsed again as if to say *hey, don't forget about me!* I unclenched my jaw, relaxed my fists, and took a deep breath.

"Listen, I'm in town for a little while. I'm going to

leave the phone number where I'm staying. If you change your mind, call me."

I waited as my mother scribbled something on the other side of my door. A scrap of paper with a series of numbers slithered under the door. I recognized her hand-writing instantly.

"Please take care of yourself. And call me."

I closed my eyes and tried to steady my breathing as her footsteps receded. Great. Karen Marquette weaseling back into my life had not been on my Bingo card. I tucked the scrap of paper into my pocket, my face burning with anger. At Gran's funeral, where she was a no-show, my uncles told me they thought she was living with some spiritualist commune in Colorado. My mother had tried to re-enter my life before when she got sober, once when I was in high school and once when Star was born. She never stayed clean long, though, and after my experience with Eric, I had a hard time trusting people again. Especially addicts. But now, with Grandma Maddie gone and so many unsettling things happening, my heart softened.

"Wait."

I opened the door and called out to the figure walking down my driveway. It had been nearly thirteen years since I last saw my mother, and she looked about the same, if not a little more worn around the edges. Her hair was a dark box-dyed brunette, but a line of silver roots told me she would no doubt be fully gray otherwise. Karen Marquette looked like me but more weathered, the skin on her face and chest a tanned hide from too much sun and too many cigarettes. Her eyes were exactly like mine, though. Hollowed. Haunted.

"It's been a long time," she said. "It's good to see you."

"What do you want?" I crossed my arms at my chest.

"Is my granddaughter here?"

"It's a school day. She'll be home later this afternoon."

"Oh." She paused. "Well, I'll make this quick. Can I come in?"

"Sure." I opened the door wider, bracing myself as she walked up to my front porch, her cheap flip-flops slapping against the cement. We did not hug.

"Looks like a dang time capsule in here," she said, her gaze zeroing in on the credenza. "Welp, there it is. I never thought I would see that cursed thing again."

"You could have seen it plenty of times if you ever visited Gran." I moved to the kitchen. "Coffee?"

"I'll have some if you're having some." My mother sat at the dining room table and groaned as she eased into the chair. "Mom wouldn't have known who I was. Even so, she wouldn't have wanted to see me anyway."

"She would have known you were there. Just because she didn't remember everything doesn't mean she wasn't all there."

I poured two cups of coffee and placed one in front of her, my chest tight with anxiety and pent-up anger. I chose to remain standing, holding the other cup of coffee near my pounding heart like a security blanket.

"So, what brings you here?" I asked.

"Your safety," she said, taking a sip of coffee. "You and Star. I want you to be safe."

"What makes you think we aren't safe?"

Mom snickered into her cup and hitched a thumb toward the credenza. "That thing there. It's cursed."

I took a thoughtful sip of coffee, trying to figure out how to respond. My mother wasn't known for being trustworthy. I had an idea why she would have come sniffing around, though.

"You know, I told your Uncle Jimmy not to let Mom take that thing with her to the nursing home. I told them to destroy it or at least get it far away from our family. Of course, he and your Uncle Mike never believe anything I have to say."

"Why do you think the cabinet is cursed?"

"Because I've seen what it can do. Bad things happen to people because of that hunk of cursed wood," she said, pulling out a purple pack of 305s cigarettes.

I pinched the bridge of my nose. A headache was coming on. Of course, my mother would come around spouting nonsense and wasting my time instead of trying to reconnect. In a perfect world, I would iron things out with my mother and try to form some kind of relationship, but all she ever did was make my blood pressure rise.

"I know, I know. You don't believe me either. But you will."

"Mom, I really have to get back to work…"

"There was a book in one of the drawers when I was a kid. Hidden. It had the most awful pictures in it. I couldn't read the words, but I know the work of the Devil when I see it."

My blood chilled as I remembered the book in my grandmother's cardboard box. I had dismissed it as some vintage recipe book, something Grandma Maddie had forgotten about. That couldn't be what my crazy mother was talking about, could it?

Her eyebrows raised as she read my expression. "You've seen the book, haven't you?"

I sighed and rolled my eyes. "Mom, it's just a stupid piece of furniture."

"No, it's not. It's dangerous."

"Well, what do you think I should do about it?"

"Get it out of your house," she said. "I'll do it for you."

My gaze flicked to the two business cards on the kitchen counter—one from Dietzer and one from the police officer. The anger from my chest flushed up to my face as I realized what my mother was trying to get at.

"You know about Dietzer, don't you? Is that what this is about? You're trying to sell the credenza for yourself."

"He was here?" The cigarette dangling from her lips fell to the table.

"Yeah, but it seems like you already knew that." I picked up her purse and her pack of cigarettes. "You can have your cigarette outside. We're done here."

"Whatever you do, *do not* sell the cabinet to that man. He's in on it! He's pure evil!" My mother stood up and followed me to the front door. "Veronica, listen to me. I know we haven't spoken for a long time, but please believe that I only want the best for you and—"

"Goodbye, Mother. Please don't come back uninvited again."

I shoved the purse into her chest and held the door open as she reluctantly stepped into the afternoon light. Her eyes were watery, and her voice sounded less assured than before. She seemed shaky. Spooked.

"Veronica," she said, pulling out her lighter. "I really do love you."

"I know, Mom."

I shut the door.

Chapter Nine

VERONICA

WHEN I WAS certain that my mother was gone, I went out to my shed and dug out the cardboard box filled with my grandmother's things. I hadn't planned on going through the items in the box until I was caught up with some of my work, but after my unexpected visit, I couldn't resist the pull. My finger throbbed as I carried the cardboard box into the house and rummaged through the contents on my kitchen table. As my hand closed around the book, my injured fingertip grazed something sharp.

"Fuck!" I pulled my hand out of the box. A thin trickle of blood dripped from my splinter wound all the way down to my wrist. I grabbed a paper towel from the kitchen and dabbed at my finger before dumping the contents of the box out on the table. I had forgotten about the knife.

"What a stupid, careless thing to do, Veronica." I picked up the horn-handled dagger and wiped a small smudge of my blood from the blade. "Great, now I'll probably get tetanus, too."

I stuck my bloody finger in my mouth, placed the knife on the table, and picked up the book. It was a hardcover bound in green book cloth with a word on the spine that I didn't recognize. *Voorschrift.*

I opened the cover, intoxicated by the vellichor aroma of decomposing paper, ink, and glue. Just as I had suspected, the words inside the book were written in a foreign language, too. At first glance, it looked like any other mid-century book you might find at a thrift store, but upon further inspection, I realized it was something else entirely. There was no copyright page nor any credit to an author or publisher. But there were photographs and illustrations.

Lots of illustrations.

As I turned the pages, it became clear to me why my mother thought the book was evil. The vintage photos and illustrations depicted in the book were ghastly. Unspeakable. With every turn of the page, I was exposed to graphic images of men and women of all ages and shapes, stripped bare and laid out, their insides on the outside. Platters of intestines. Tureens of indistinguishable organs. Even though I didn't understand the words on the page, the format and contents made it clear that what I was reading was some kind of human cookbook.

"Oh, fuck no!" I slammed the book shut at the last photograph, a severed head on a plate with the eyes and tongue laid out on a sprig of green lettuce like some kind of fucked up garnish. Hot bile rushed up my throat, causing me to choke and aspirate as the familiar image of the severed head and its hollowed eyes burned into my brain. I turned to the kitchen sink and heaved out the rest of my stomach contents, my lungs burning as I coughed and retched.

I wiped my mouth and returned to the kitchen table. *Why the fuck did Grandma Maddie have a book like that?* Where did she even get it? I glanced over my shoulder at the whine of school bus brakes in the distance. Star was due to be home any minute. I couldn't let her see my grandmother's fucked up version of *Mastering the Art of French Cooking.* Shaking, I stuffed all of the items back into the box and placed them back on the credenza. My throbbing finger was now becoming unbearable. I wrapped the reopened wound with a band-aid.

Star flopped on the couch as soon as she got home and dozed off while I finished cleaning up my work for the day. As she napped, I contemplated what to do with the contents of the box. I didn't want to get rid of my grandmother's things, but now, everything next to that book seemed tainted. Poisoned. The thought of keeping the book in my home another moment longer gave me the creeps.

When Star awoke from her nap, she presented me with a pile of paperwork. The first week of school always meant filling out tons of forms, and this year was no exception. With every push of the ink pen, my fingertip ached, and I knew that a trip to urgent care was becoming more imminent. I didn't have the time or money to take care of my wound properly. Moms aren't allowed to be sick, especially single moms. I was going to have to defrost the frozen block of ice that encased the credit card I vowed never to use again. I had stashed the card in the freezer after paying it off, promising myself only to use it in case of an emergency. But from the look and feel of my swollen, throbbing finger, things were only going to get worse.

"I'm hungry. What's for dinner?" Star asked, flopping down next to me at the dining room table.

"I can make that Thai curry you like," I said, filling out the last bit of paperwork. "Or maybe just sandwiches. I don't know how much longer I can use my hand. This cut on my finger hurts like hell."

"Hey, what's this?"

I looked up from the school clinic card I was filling out to see Star, her face screwed up in a disgusted expression with the *Voorschrift* open in front of her.

"No! Star, that's not—"

"Sick!" Star looked at me in confusion as I snatched the book from her hands. "What is that?"

"A bad book written by bad people." I reached under the table and pulled out the box. "I didn't mean for you to see that."

"Was that Grandma Maddie's book?" Star said, her voice thin. "Why would she have that?"

"I asked myself the same question." I tossed the book back in the box. "I don't know. I think maybe it's connected to that cabinet somehow."

"The credenza."

"Yeah. Maybe when she bought it, the book was

already in there? I don't know. This sort of thing would have disgusted her just as much."

"Why did you keep it?" Star asked, hugging her arms to her chest. "I don't think I'm hungry anymore."

"I just found it right before you got home," I said. "I didn't mean for you to see it. I was going to get rid of it."

Star's eyes locked with mine. "We should burn it."

I nodded. "I agree."

I followed Star to the backyard with the book pinched between my fingers and held away from my body as if it was covered in dog shit. We had a small fire pit set up for chilly evenings made of old land-scaping bricks, perfect for roasting marshmallows or, in this case, incinerating cursed books. Star got lighter fluid and matches from where we kept them near the grill on our back porch. I tossed the book into the center of our pit, filled with old ashes and half-burned logs.

"Do you think that the pictures in there are real?" Star whispered, staring at the book.

I shook my head. "I don't know. But I don't want to look at them anymore."

"Me neither."

I flipped the cap of the lighter fluid and doused the book with a quarter of the bottle. Then I put my hand out. "Matches."

Star handed me the box.

I picked out a match, struck it on the side, and lowered the flame to the book. Before I had another chance to react, the book suddenly combusted into a burst of bright orange, and a trail of fire snaked up from the pit to my arm, engulfing my finger in flame.

———

"How on Earth did you manage to burn just one finger?" The nurse at urgent care chuckled and gave me an incredulous look as she bandaged up my hand.

"Cooking dinner." I glanced at Star under heavy brows.

Star nodded. "Yeah. Mom's not so great in the kitchen."

"Hey, I'm trying." I let out a low, half-crazed laugh. "You know, I already had a wound on that finger? I got a splinter earlier in the week, and it got infected and —nevermind."

"Well, you're all patched up now." The nurse gave me a condescending pat on top of my hand. "Try to remember to wear oven mitts next time."

"Noted. Thank you." I pursed my lips and glanced at Star. "Come on. Let's go."

Cleanse it with fire.

I glanced over my shoulder and jumped at the whispery voice. Star gave me one of her skeptical looks.

"Did you say something?" I asked.

She shook her head. "No."

"Weird," I said. "This place gives me the ick. Let's get outta here."

Star and I didn't say a word as we left the urgent care clinic and drove home. There wasn't much to say. We both tried to burn a book of ritualistic human cannibal-ism, and I ended up getting burned instead. What else do you do after that but get something to eat?

"Well, I had to break the seal on the Visa in the freez-er," I finally said. "Might as well make a night of it. Wanna go get dinner somewhere?"

"Olive Garden?"

I cringed. It was her favorite restaurant, but certainly not mine. "Sure."

I pulled into the chain restaurant, and Star and I filled up on salad and breadsticks. Neither of us wanted to talk about what happened as we twirled noodles around our forks. I was relieved to have Star download her day at school on me instead, gladly listening to her report of who was dating who, who gossiped about who, and what new pair of shoes she wanted to get.

When we returned home, it was nearly 11 pm, way past bedtime. Star skipped her shower and fell into bed with her clothes on, sneakers and all. Despite having a belly full of carbonara, I was not nearly as tired as I should have been. I couldn't stop thinking about the book. The credenza. My fucked up mother. Ever since Grandma Maddie died, everything felt unbalanced. Weird. It was certainly grief taking hold, but my instincts told me there was something more at play. Only what, I didn't know.

I grabbed my flashlight and headed out to the back-yard to finish the job. We had left in a hurry after the lighter fluid accident, and I needed to make sure that the book had been destroyed. Being in possession of something like that felt dangerous, like an assault on my senses, not to mention probably illegal. The depictions in the book looked alarmingly realistic and lifelike, and with no publisher to account for, it was hard to tell if what they depicted was fake or real.

The atmosphere pressed in on me from all sides, smothering me in a blanket of humid, damp, and dark. The air smelled of burnt cinders and rotten earth, and everything was quiet and still, unnaturally so, as though someone had muted all of the bugs and creatures of the night. I heard only my heartbeat hammering in my ears as I approached the cold fire pit. I had hoped to see a pile of burning embers, pages blackened to the point of being unreadable. But what I saw in the darkened fire pit was even more chilling. The book wasn't burned to ashes, reduced to a pile of charged pages.

The book was gone.

Chapter Ten

VERONICA

"So, you think someone came into our backyard and stole the book?"

Star chewed on a granola bar in the passenger seat the following morning as I drove her to school. My eyes were red and scratchy from lack of sleep, and my head didn't feel much better either. I had stayed up all night trying to find any kind of information on the book or the makers of the credenza but came up with nothing.

"Either that or it walked off on its own," I said. "I don't know which scenario creeps me out more."

"Maybe we should get a camera for the backyard, too," Star said.

I winced. "I know. I'm sorry I haven't done it yet. I'll use the credit card and pick up some cameras today."

"Thank you."

"You know, it was probably just your grandma," I

said. "I wouldn't doubt if she was the one who broke into our backyard and took it."

"Why would she take it though?"

I shook my head. "Who knows? She kept talking about wanting to keep us safe when she came by. She mentioned that she knew about the book. My mother is sick, but she means well."

"So why don't you ever want to see her?"

"Because she's dangerous." I clenched my jaw, holding back the words. How honest do you get with your twelve-year-old daughter? "I don't think she would ever hurt us, but there's a reason she didn't raise me."

"Am I going to end up like her?" Star looked at me from under a waterfall of faded purple hair. "Are you?"

A knife stuck in my heart. "No, babe. Why would you think that?"

"I read that mental health issues are sometimes inherited," she said. "Grandma Maddie was sick. Your mom is sick. What about us?"

I let out a sigh and gave her knee a reassuring pat. "We won't let that happen. We'll look out for each other and get some help if we need it. Okay?"

She gave me a weary, half-hearted smile. "Okay."

Guilt rested like a stone on my shoulders as I dropped Star off at school and waved goodbye. I felt like I was somehow responsible for the strange series of events that had been occurring, the heavy weight of our reality. I didn't want her to feel scared or anxious in her own home; it was a sensation I was all too intimate with. I tensed up and clutched the steering wheel. I wasn't looking forward to charging yet another necessary item on my previously paid-off credit card. It wasn't until I reached a stoplight that I realized I was still gripping the wheel hard. I glanced down at my bandaged hand, and that's when it hit me.

My finger didn't hurt anymore.

"That nurse must have used some strong ointment." I cocked my head to the side and tore at the fabric tape and cotton gauze. I pulled off the bandage and gazed down at my finger, completely mystified.

Cleanse it with fire.

No burn. No cut mark. It was completely healed. What gives?

HONK!

I jumped out of my skin and glanced up at the green stoplight. My gaze flicked to the rearview, where a man was frantically waving his hands for me to move along.

"Sorry, jeeze."

I let my foot off the brake and accelerated. I knew I needed to buy the security cameras as soon as possible, but there were too many questions floating around my head. I needed some answers first before I dug into my next project of DIY home security installation. I needed to go to the library.

My phone buzzed as I pulled into downtown toward the library parking lot. Fernando's number blazed across my screen, and I smiled.

F: I'm bringing ingredients to make my famous chicken alfredo tomorrow. You're not a vegetarian, right?

I parked and grabbed my phone. Did I even remember how to flirt? I guess I was about to find out.

V: Don't worry I'm not afraid-o anything you want to cook.

I groaned and immediately wished I could unsend my bad attempt at a joke. Thankfully, Fernando gave me a gracious smiley-face laughing emoji in response.

F: Okay, see you Friday then.

I sat in the parking lot for a few moments, staring at the library in a daze. What was I doing with Fernando? He was a nice guy to talk to at the assisted living center, but I never really considered him romantically. I'd gone on a few dates here and there over the years with men I'd met at weekend markets or in the resale community, but none of them lasted long. After Eric, it seemed like romance was something I just wasn't interested in anymore. If I was being honest, this thing with Fernando felt rushed and forced on my end. Still, I knew I needed to try to get out there. I couldn't rely on Star to be my only source of human connection.

I shook off my self-pity, grabbed my tote bag, and exited the cool interior of my car. The early morning heat wrapped around me like a wet blanket, itchy and suffocating all at once. The library was a beautiful brick building over a hundred years old, probably the only remaining original building downtown. It looked tired and dark, shaded by old oaks, their branches dripping with coarse gray Spanish moss like witches' hair. It was refreshing to be near a place so old and rich with history among the glittering new construction of downtown.

It had been a long time since I had to do any kind of

deep library research, but I walked inside, hopeful someone would help. The furniture store that my grand-mother bought the credenza from must have closed sometime in the 1960s, making it difficult to find the name. I got a hit from the Facebook page of our local historical society, and the enthusiastic members of the group seemed to think that the place was called either Stuckies or Price Cutters. I crossed my fingers and hoped that this branch of the library would have the local history resources I needed.

A young person in glasses with a half-shaved head sat behind the information desk. I walked up to them and offered up a pitiful smile.

"Hi," I said, glancing at their nameplate on the desk. "Jules. Um, I need some information on a local business. Like historical information."

Jules put the book down they were reading and offered a warm smile. "Do you know the name?"

"It's either Stuckies or Price Cutters," I said. "I'm really not sure."

"You need the local archives," they said, pointing down a corridor. "Just over there. To the left."

"Thanks."

Thirty minutes later, I was pouring over 60-year-old photos, images, and news articles from my hometown. Places that used to be cow pastures and dirt roads were now fast-food restaurants and middle schools. Downtown Fort Myers looked completely different after some mayor gave the green light to raze the historical blocks. Finally, I found a news article about the grand opening of a furniture store called Stuckies, located only two miles from my grandmother's home. The owner was Raymond Andersen, a furniture dealer from Pennsylvania.

"Raymond Andersen," I muttered under my breath, the name ringing a bell. "Where did you get that damned piece of furniture from anyway?"

SLAM.

I jumped as one of the massive binders fell from a nearby shelf. I stood to pick up the book and return it to its rightful place when I noticed the open page. The book that had fallen was full of articles from the News-Press, this one from the year 1963. The headline staring up at me made my breath catch in my throat.

LOCAL FURNITURE DEALER FOUND DEAD

November 30, 1963

Raymond Andersen, 27, of Philadelphia, PA, a local businessman and father of two, was found decapitated at his furniture store, Stuckies, on Pondella Road, Friday, November 29th, just after 8:00 am. Andersen's family reported him missing on Thanksgiving Day, and the following morning, his remains were discovered at his place of business. Authorities are asking anyone with information regarding this case to contact the Lee County Sheriff's Department. Raymond is survived by his wife, Inez, and their two daughters.

Underneath the headline was a headshot of Raymond Andersen paired with a photo of the Stuckies furniture storefront. He looked like a nice man. Who could have done such a thing? I took out my phone and snapped a photo of the front page. If the Andersen family was still in the area, they might be able to give me some more information, but then again, they might not want to talk to some stranger about their dead grandpa, either.

I glanced at the time on my phone and realized it was getting late. I still needed to get to the store, buy security cameras, and get some of my work done for the day. I returned all the archival material to its place and stopped by the information desk on my way out.

"Find everything you need?" Jules asked.

"Yeah, I did. Thanks," I said. "Could you help me look up one more thing? I'm trying to find out some information on an old book."

"What's the author's name?"

"I don't know, actually. It's a weird book in a foreign language. It was called '*Voorschrift.*'"

"One sec. How do you spell that?"

"V-O-O-R-S-C-H-R-I-F-T."

"Got it." Jules tapped on their keyboard and scanned the computer before giving me a shake of their head. "Nope. Nothing comes up."

"That's what I thought. Thanks, have a good day."

The interior of my car was a warm oven that I was grateful to bake in after sitting for so long in the chilly library. I sat behind the wheel for a moment with my eyes closed and just breathed, letting the heat seep into my skin.

That cabinet is dangerous.

My mother's words rattled around in my brain. Maybe she was right. Or maybe things just happen, and people like to connect the dots and mold situations into their own narrative.

I opened my eyes and stuck my key in the ignition, and that's when I saw it. Well, I felt it. The sensation that someone was watching me. I gazed back at the library's windows overlooking the parking lot. To the far left of the entrance, near the area where I had been studying archives, a face stared back at me. The face of my grandmother. I held her gaze for a moment, too terrified to move. And then, just as quickly as her image materialized, it vanished again, and I was left sitting behind the wheel in tears.

———

The sun had begun to set by the time I finished tightening the last screw in our home security system. The process of installing the cameras wasn't as difficult or expensive as I thought, and I honestly felt a little silly I hadn't gotten anything like it sooner. But that was me, barely able to keep up with everyday life. My responses to things were always reactive and rarely proactive. "Maybe someday I'll get my shit together" was my motto. In the meantime, I had a daughter to protect and a business to run. If whoever had trespassed in my back-yard to take the book returned, I would get a recording of them.

I went back in the house to find Star lounging on the couch, eating macaroni and cheese.. The smell of radioactive yellow powdered sauce and pasta hit my nose and my stomach gave out an audible complaint. I had been so busy and on edge, I had forgotten to eat all day.

"Okay, so this app will alert me if anyone is at our front or back door." I handed Star my phone. "It will make a little dinging sound if someone is within range."

"Cool." Star glanced at our new front door camera. "What happens if someone tries to break in or something?"

"Then we call 9-1-1," I said. "But you don't have to worry about that. I bet these cameras will scare off any intruders. Besides, there's this siren button I can push if I see someone suspicious getting too close."

"What's this?"

Star held my phone screen out to face me. She had somehow swiped to my photo album. Raymond Andersen's good-natured smile stared back at me.

"That," I said, snatching my phone back, "is none of your business."

"It said he was beheaded. Mom, does this have something to do with that weird book?"

I gave Star a half-smile, half-frown. She was too smart for her own good. "Maybe. That was the guy who sold Grandma Maddie the credenza. I was trying to research the furniture store at the library and find someone to talk to about where it came from. That's where I found that news article."

I decided to leave out the part where I imagined seeing the ghost of my grandmother in the window. Again. No need to put any ideas into Star's already worried mind.

"Anyway, I'm still thinking about selling the cabinet to that Dietzer guy. The more I look at it, the more it creeps me out."

"Really?"

"Yeah, I mean. We obviously need the money," I said. "It's hard to let go of, though. So many memories are attached to it."

"I wish you would. It creeps me out, too." Star yawned. "Is it still okay if Dad takes me out for pizza tomorrow?"

Fuck. I'd forgotten about that. And about Fernando coming over.

"That's fine." I sighed. "I feel like I should cancel with Fernando. I'm not really in the mood to hang out with anyone."

"*Mom.*" Star's eyes rolled to the back of her head. "When was the last time you went out on a date?"

"It's not a date."

"Or did anything fun with a friend?" Star glared at me. "You're going to get weird if you don't hang out with other people."

"I *do* hang out with other people!"

"Work stuff doesn't count," she said. "Come on. It's just Fernando. He's nice."

"I don't think that I even like him that way. It doesn't feel right to lead him on."

"So just be friends," Star said. "No big deal."

"It doesn't always work that way." I sighed again. "Tell your dad you can go out for pizza. Speaking of food, I need to go find something to eat."

The rest of the evening was a blur of chores, television, and routine. I helped Star with her homework, and when she went to bed, I brewed a pot of coffee and got to work on my inventory. After my research at the library, installing the security system, and spending time with Star, I hadn't had a chance to get my regular work done.

I sat behind my desk and looked around at the plastic bins filled with vintage clothing, jewelry, and collectibles surrounding me that still needed to be cataloged on my website. I didn't have the energy or enthusiasm to do any of it. I glanced down at my healed fingertip and considered it might be time to pack up shop. Maybe I could work at the library. Jules seemed nice. I could say hi to the ghost of my grandma now and then and....

No. I walked to the bathroom, turned the faucet on cold, and splashed my face in the sink. I'd been through tougher times than this before and always figured out a way to make things work. Refurbishing and recycling old things made me happy, and besides, running my own business was a point of pride.

"Suck it up, Veronica." I took a sip of coffee. "No one is coming to save you."

I fired up my laptop, determined to get my head back in the game. A few sales or inquiries from potential buyers would have helped to boost my spirits. Unfortunately, my work email inbox was nearly empty, with the exception of one very strange message.

To: info@veronicasvintage

From: xeyzi09jkle1@embark.de
Subject: (empty)

I figured the email missed my spam folder somehow, but curiosity got the best of me, and I opened it anyway. What I saw on the screen before me made my pulse speed up. Someone had sent a series of PDF pages ripped from vintage magazines and news articles. The first was from a Southern Living article from the early 1960s featuring Raymond Andersen. In the article, Raymond is proudly standing in front of a credenza. *My* credenza.

Stuckies Brings Danish Style to South Florida

Raymond Andersen knows a thing or two about traditional Danish style. His father grew up in a village just outside of Copen-hagen, carving tables and chairs by hand before moving to Pennsyl-vania nearly fifty years ago. Now, with the help of his cousin, craftsman Lars Andersen, the duo are bringing European styling to South Floridian homes. Andersen's boutique furniture store, Stuckies, is set to open in the spring and will carry fine furniture for the modern home.

The other attached PDF was even more cryptic and featured a newspaper article written in what I could only guess was Dutch. The article didn't tell me much, but I was able to recognize one of the names: Lars Andersen. I used a translation app to try and figure out some of the words. The word *vermoord* stood out from the text. So did the word *onthoofd*. Murdered. Beheaded.

The hair stood up on the back of my arms as I closed the email.

Both Andersen men met the same grisly fate—intimately connected to my grandmother's credenza. Was someone trying to scare me into getting rid of the cabinet? Perhaps it really was a rare enough piece of furniture that some collector would pay an unreasonable amount of money for it. Whoever was feeding me this information wanted me to connect the dots and figure out I wasn't just dealing with some old hunk of junk. There was something very strange about the history behind my grandmother's credenza; that much was clear. Only what, I wasn't quite sure.

Chapter Eleven

VERONICA

"Okay if we go see a movie after dinner?"

It was Friday afternoon, and Eric's Jeep was idling in my driveway again. He had come to pick up Star for their pizza dinner date, as promised and on time. His eyes were clear; he looked clean and well-rested. I couldn't say no.

"Yeah, just not too late."

"You doin' okay?"

The question caught me by surprise. Even during the short time we were together, he never seemed to be in tune with my emotions. Granted, I hadn't slept well lately for obvious reasons, and I'm sure the stress showed in my pinched expression and dark under-eye circles. I tucked a strand of hair behind my ear and nodded, perhaps a little too enthusiastically.

"Yeah. I'm great."

"It's just that, well, Star said you were having some

money problems." Eric shifted in his seat. "I feel bad. I know I owe you big time. I'm trying to make up for it, really."

"Well, yeah. You do owe me." I chuckled. "We're fine, though."

"I started a college fund for Star through my work. Did she tell you that?"

"No." Adrenaline shot up my legs. *College.* I wasn't ready to think about that. "That's really nice though."

"Yeah, you know. She's a smart kid; she deserves it." Eric cleared his throat. "Anyway, I know you're probably too sore at me still or too proud to ask or whatever. But I got a solid job now. Anything you need for Star, you let me know. I wanna help."

"I appreciate that."

The front door slammed, and Star bounded down the front steps. She wrapped her arms around my waist from behind and gave me a squeeze before running to the passenger side door.

"Bye, Mom."

"Bye, babe."

I still had mixed feelings about sharing my daughter with Eric again. He missed all of her firsts, all of the sleepless nights of early parenting. All the good times and the bad. I often wondered what our life would have been like if Eric hadn't lost himself. Maybe Star would have been a daddy's girl. Maybe Eric and I would have gotten married too young and then divorced anyway. There was no use in pondering over maybes.

Eric waved goodbye, and my phone buzzed in my

back pocket. I glanced at the screen to see Fernando's name.

F: On my way. Be there in 15.

Shit. A quick whiff of my underarms told me I needed to freshen up. I had already done the full shower, shave, and hair blowout prep that morning, but I was still dressed in my work clothes. I sped to my bedroom and picked out a blue floral vintage A-line dress I had scored from a yard sale. By the time I dressed, reapplied my deodorant, and checked my makeup, there was a knock at the door.

It's just Fernando. It doesn't have to be a date.

"Hi!" I said, perhaps a little too enthusiastically as I opened the door. My body posture felt awkward and weird as I opened the door wider. "Come on in."

"Hey." Fernando smiled, a fabric grocery bag pressed to his chest. "You're quite the interior decorator."

"Thanks." I shut the door and smoothed my hair.

Fernando looked nice with his dark hair combed back and a crisp, fitted black t-shirt. He smelled good, too. A heavy beat of silence passed between us, and I realized I was staring. I blinked and cleared my throat. "Can I get you a glass of wine?"

"Maybe in a little bit," he said. "Is Star here?"

"No. She went to get pizza. With her dad." I held out my hand for the grocery bag. "Want me to take that?"

"Yeah."

Fernando made himself comfortable in the kitchen and unpacked the grocery bag as I struggled to engage in small talk. I poured myself a glass of wine and sipped as he filled me in on the gossip from Herons Glen and some recent car troubles he'd had. After I downed my first glass of wine, I loosened up a bit. Fernando asked how Star was doing in school and how things were going with her father. I poured myself another glass.

"So things between you and your ex are cool now?"

"I wouldn't say *cool*." I took a sip of wine. "We're civil, though. I'm trying to make things work for Star's sake."

"It's gotta be hard raising a kid on your own," he said. "And expensive."

"It is. That's one of the reasons why I'm considering selling the cabinet to that guy."

"The one who was going to pay big money for it?"

"Did I tell you about that?" I asked.

"You must have," he shrugged. "Someone wanted to buy it for a bunch of money, right?"

"Yeah."

"Sounds like a good deal to me," Fernando said. "I know your grandma loved it, but it's just a piece of furniture. No offense."

"No, you're right. I should just let it go and sell it."

"What's holding you back?"

I took a deep breath and thought about his question. *What was stopping me?* It wasn't like me to be this indecisive. Up until the last few months, I was barely getting by. It was easy to blame my flightiness on grief, but I couldn't deny that there was something else at play.

"The deal sounds too good to be true, I guess. Ten

grand is a lot to pay for a piece of furniture like that." I shrugged. "Plus, some weird stuff has been happening."

"What kind of weird stuff?"

I looked at him, unsure how much I should tell him about what was going on. "I got a strange email about the credenza from an unknown person. I don't know… my nutcase mother probably sent it to me to try and scare me. She thinks the cabinet is cursed."

"Cursed?" Fernando chuckled. "Why would she think that?"

"She thinks a lot of things. When she was a teenager, she heard voices. After I was born, it got worse. She started taking drugs to quiet the inner dialogue in her head. I don't know. I should feel bad for her. She's my mother, and she's clearly unwell, but I have a lot of bad memories because of her."

Fernando nodded and listened as he cooked. "Weird stuff and bad memories. All the more reason to get rid of the cabinet if you ask me."

"You're right."

"So there you go. Problem solved."

"I think what's really holding me back is that I don't want to sell it just because I need the money. I know it's my pride talking, but I don't want to have to get a job and give up on my business. I've worked so hard, and I'm going through a rough patch, is all. I don't want to look back in a few years and regret selling the cabinet just because I couldn't make ends meet."

"I don't know. I would have a hard time turning down ten grand. But I guess I get it."

A heavy silence fell between us as Fernando continued to cook. Something felt off. The casual, friendly banter we had always shared felt miles away, though our conversations were never that deep. Maybe this is why I wasn't able to make friends. I never opened up or shared anything, and when I did, it was always too much.

"We can totally talk about something else, by the way," I said, gulping my wine. "I'm not trying to dump on you or anything."

"It's okay." Fernando cut a piece of cheese from the block he bought. He hovered near me, so close I could feel the heat radiating off his skin. He held the cheese to my lips, his dark gaze locking with mine. "Try this. It will go with your wine."

Fernando gave me a wry grin as he tried to feed me the cheese. Even though we had been casual friends for a long time, this setting felt very much like the makings of a date, and the gesture was too intimate for me. I plucked the cheese from his fingers and popped it into my mouth.

"See? It's good, right?"

"Thanks." My stomach flipped, and not in a nervous, flirty sort of way. I backed up and took a seat at the table as Fernando finished cooking our meal, suddenly turned off by the entire scenario. An unsettling sensation had wormed its way into my gut—the same kind of feeling one gets when walking alone in a dark parking lot at night. It was a hollow, vulnerable sensation, like being at the bottom of a dark pit with no way out. Having a first date at my home had been a bad idea. We should have gone out for coffee or dinner or even a movie. *How much did I really even know about Fernando?* He could do anything to me, and Star wouldn't be home for hours.

"Everything okay?" Fernando glared at me under heavy eyebrows, his full lips turned down.

What am I thinking? This is my friend! Fernando wouldn't hurt me. I was letting my anxiety get the best of me. Either way, I had to admit that my feelings for him weren't in the least bit romantic. Time to change the subject.

"Yeah, I'm fine. Sorry. There's something else, though. Something I haven't told anyone."

"Ooh, secrets." Fernando began to plate up dinner. "What is it? Are you really a spy?"

"There was a book in the box of my grandma's things you saved. And a knife. They were both weird. Do you remember seeing them back at Herons Glen?"

"No, but I didn't pack up the box," Fernando said, bringing our plates to the table. "I just held it to the side for you."

"Here, let me show you." I went to the credenza and pulled out the paper-wrapped knife. I turned and showed it to Fernando, and his expression went slack.

"That thing looks dangerous."

"It is. It cut me once already." I extended the knife in his direction. "It's heavy. Here, feel it."

"No, thanks." Fernando held his hands up in a defensive way. "I don't want to touch that."

"Oh. Sorry." The air felt heavy between us as I realized I messed up again.

"It's fine. It's just our dinner is getting cold." Fernando motioned to the table.

"You're right." I cringed and wrapped the knife back up in paper. I was ruining the night. He didn't want to hear about the weird things that were happening to me. After the way Fernando looked at the knife, I decided to keep what happened with the book to myself.

I sat back down at the table, picked up my fork and knife, and forced a smile.

"Thanks. This looks great."

―――――

Fernando and I shared a strained meal, punctuated by clipped conversation and the scraping of silverware against plates. I faked a headache, and he politely left after we cleaned up. To tell the truth, I was relieved he didn't stay longer. I hadn't been looking for romance, and I wasn't really in the mood for romance to find me. I did want a friend, but I wouldn't blame Fernando for not wanting to contact me again after our awkward dinner.

If I took one thing away from my disaster date, it was that I didn't want to get rid of the credenza. I also realized that I didn't want to lose my business. I needed to quit obsessing over whatever perceived weirdness was going on and stop trying to connect dots that didn't exist. It was time to get out of my own head, buckle down, and get back on track.

Star was all smiles as she returned home, just as I was finishing up the dishes. I was happy to see that she was happy, and relieved that Eric was continuing to keep good on his word. Star greeted me with a hug and kiss, the scent of buttered movie theater popcorn on her breath.

"How was the movie?"

"It was okay. Some action flick about a bunch of middle-aged guys." Star tossed her purse on the counter. "How did your date go?"

"Not great," I admitted. "Fernando is a nice guy, but I think it's best if we stay friends."

"Really? That's too bad. I like him."

"I do, too," I said. "Nothing romantic is going to happen, though. There's no spark."

"Dad was asking about you."

"That's *definitely* not going to happen."

"Not like *that*." Star rolled her eyes. "He was just saying you should come over for Thanksgiving dinner, too. If you want."

"Oh." I blinked, taken aback. "Well, that's a nice offer, but it might be weird."

"Grandma will be nice to you. Dad says she still likes you better than him."

"I bet." I laughed. "I'll think about it. Tell him thank you for the offer."

"I'm going to bed." Star pecked me on the cheek and turned toward the hall. "Night."

"G'night."

After Star closed her bedroom door, I poured the rest of the wine bottle into my glass. I listened to the silence of my home, straining my ears to hear something, anything. I stared at my grandmother's cabinet. I could feel it staring back.

"What do you want from me?"

The credenza didn't answer.

I crossed the room and ran my hands along the smooth wooden top. My previously injured finger caressed the corner where my face made contact more than thirty years ago. Maybe it wasn't the cabinet that was cursed. Maybe it was just me.

I bent over and lay across the top of the cabinet, resting my cheek on the cool surface as I pressed my ear to the wood. I sucked in a slow, deep lungful of air, letting my chest press into the credenza with each rise and fall. From somewhere deep inside the solid wooden cabinet, I swore I heard the soft thrum of a heartbeat.

Chapter Twelve

MADELINE, 1967

"Karen, go back to bed!"

It was a Saturday evening in November, and Madeline Marquette was on her knees on the dining room floor, scrubbing vomit from the shag carpet. Her youngest child and only daughter, Karen, stood in the hallway outside her bedroom door, rubbing sleep from her eyes. One more step and Karen would have stuck her bare foot into a pile of Evelyn Fontaine's barfed-up shrimp appetizer.

"What's that smell?" Karen whined.

"It's nothing. Get back to bed."

Madeline blew a strand of hair from her face that had fallen loose from her perfectly coiffed bouffant. The aroma of bile and stomach contents rose from the carpet in hot, steamy vapors. She gagged and stood up. "Seriously, honey. It's not safe for you to be out here."

"Okay." Karen yawned, returned to her bedroom, and shut the door.

Madeline stifled a sob as she looked back down at her ruined carpet. All her hard work, all of her planning and cooking and entertaining, paid back in piles of vomit. One minute, she and her friends were eating and drinking while gossiping about who was stepping out with who after Wednesday night bridge. The next minute, all of her guests were violently ill at the same time. Madeline knew she wasn't the best cook, but she was clean, and she made sure to use the freshest of ingredients. Now, the entire neighborhood would be gossiping about her and how she gave half the Pondella Bridge Club food poisoning.

All she wanted to do was make friends. Since Eddie died, Madeline had been so lonely. The friends they had shared as a couple slowly faded away because they no longer knew how to support her grief. Either that, or the wives were afraid she might seek comfort from their husbands. The other mothers at Karen's elementary school were younger than her, and the ladies at the salon were older. Even the ladies from the nearby Baptist church stopped calling. Madeline had high hopes the bridge club would bring her some kind of fellowship, but now, her social standing with them was likely in the crapper.

Madeline finished scraping chunks from the carpet and then got to the business of dabbing out the mess. Thankfully, the rust color of her shag carpet masked any staining, but she would still have to hire someone to shampoo it. She cursed herself for thinking carpet was a good idea in her dining space. She had already learned that lesson in the bathrooms.

It was nearly midnight by the time she had finished hand-washing and drying all the fancy dishes she purchased specifically for the dinner party. She had been keeping the special porcelain plates in the credenza so the kids wouldn't chip any of the delicate edges, each dish lovingly stacked in one of the side cabinets. It was the first time she even had the opportunity to use the plates, and now, it seemed like it was the last.

When she was satisfied with her work, Madeline took the candelabra from the dining room table and placed it in the bottom drawer of the credenza where she always kept it. She tried to shut the drawer, but something caught. She slammed the drawer with a little too much force and heard something click.

"Dammit."

Madeline opened the drawer to find the frame was askew. She lifted the candelabra out and wedged her fingers between the cracks of the drawer. Her fingers closed around a false bottom. She lifted the panel away to reveal a concealed hidden space within the third drawer.

Inside that hidden space was a green clothbound book.

And a horn-handled knife.

Chapter Thirteen

VERONICA

I WAS NOT good at many things, but when it came to avoiding my problems, I had become a true pro. Undoing all the bad habits I had acquired and self-pity thought patterns took persistence, patience, and time. After my disastrous date with Fernando, I knew it was time to dig myself out of the hole of self-pity I had fallen into. Slowly, I began to crawl out of my grief and back into the life I had built for Star and myself.

The sweltering days of late summer gave way to the cool of autumn as weeks fell from the calendar. Business picked back up for Veronica's Vintage online shop, as did my outdoor vending events. I made sure to sign up for every nearby craft fair and neighborhood market I could afford to attend, and my hard work paid off. I caught up on all of my bills and stashed the emergency credit card back in the freezer where it belonged. Finally, finances weren't quite so tight. Star was happy. I was mostly happy. Life seemed to find a solid rhythm again.

The strange visions and voices I had been hearing stopped, too. There were no more surprise visits from my mother, no more cryptic emails. My home security cameras didn't pick up anyone skulking around the property. Star was thriving at school, and it felt safe to be home. It was all I could ask for.

Fernando never contacted me again after our strained dinner. I didn't blame him, and I wasn't surprised. Even if I had been in the right headspace to date, we simply weren't a good romantic match. I still got lonely at times, and I tried not to think about a future without Star in it. That kind of thinking was a path that would only lead to a deep pit of depression. I didn't want to have to climb out of it again.

Sometime in October, Star discovered a love for all things pumpkin and baking. Thankfully, she proved to be more skilled than I in the kitchen and made batch after batch of pumpkin bread, pies, and cookies. The house smelled of cinnamon and clove in the evenings when she baked, and our home felt warm and full of comfort and love.

I knew it was too good to last.

"Is it okay if I use this plate?"

It was Saturday morning, and Star had just finished baking yet another batch of pumpkin bread. Eric was on his way over to pick her up to stay overnight at his mom's house for the first time. Star was spending more and more time getting to know his side of the family and was growing closer to Eric's mother, Susan. I had always liked her and was happy for Star to have a stable grandmother to look up to.

"Where'd you get that?" I took the plate from Star and examined it, though I already knew what it was. Grandma Maddie's Carolina blue porcelain plates were in near-mint condition. I was always too afraid I would ruin them, so they stayed packed away.

"I found them in the closet. Didn't they belong to Grandma Maddie?"

"Yeah, I've been meaning to put them away in the cabinet," I said. "Why do you want to use it?"

"I wanna bring Grandma Suzy some of my pumpkin bread. This would make it look special."

I tilted my head to the side. "These are really expensive plates, you know."

"I know. I'll take good care of it."

"Okay. Just make sure it comes home with you, okay?"

"Thank you!"

I walked over to the hallway linen closet and opened the door. Sure enough, the cardboard box that housed my grandmother's plates had been opened. After I decided to keep the credenza, it had only seemed natural that the plates should be returned to their former housing. I picked up the box and took the plates to the dining table when there was a knock on the door. I glanced at my phone and pulled up the front door security camera. Eric was early.

"I got it!"

Star ran to answer the front door.

"Hey, Dad!"

Eric swooped down for a hug and met my gaze. "Hey, kid."

"Everything okay?" I asked. Eric typically waited outside. I bristled at the idea of him seeing the inside of my home.

"I hate to ask, but can I use the bathroom? It's a long drive, and I had way too much coffee this morning."

I nodded. "Star, show your dad the bathroom."

"It's over here."

I scrolled on my phone and waited as the water ran in my bathroom. The thought of my ex using my most personal space made me uncomfortable. Fortunately, Eric was fast.

"Thanks." Eric emerged from the bathroom with a warm smile. "Okay, kid, let's hit the road."

"Look what I made!" Star held the dish up, proudly displaying her pumpkin bread.

"I thought I smelled something good," Eric said. "You baked that?"

"Yep. With real pumpkin. Want a piece?"

"Naw, I'm sure your mom wants us to get on our way." Eric met my eye with an apologetic look.

"No, it's fine. I just made a fresh pot of coffee. You want some?"

Eric blinked in surprise. "Sure. Yeah, love some."

Star and Eric sat down at the dining room table as I poured the coffee. I smiled as Eric indulged Star, listening as she unloaded the last week of school and friend gossip onto him. Star gave us each a slice of pumpkin bread on a napkin as I joined them at the table.

"...and then Neveah said she had never seen *The Matrix* and that it was an old movie and it looked dumb. Can you believe that?" Star shoved a bite of pumpkin bread in her mouth. *"Mabaeh donnen no wha she talken abou."*

"Your mom and I saw *The Matrix* together on our first date," Eric said, taking a bite of pumpkin bread. "It's my favorite movie, and she had never seen it."

"I forgot about that." I took a bite of my bread, not wanting to add my own two cents. *Your dad later pawned his DVD of The Matrix and everything else we owned.* It would have been unnecessarily cruel to bring that fact up in front of Star, but it was one I didn't want to forget.

Star swallowed. "Anyway, can we watch *Kill Bill* this weekend? Mom said I was too young before, but I'm in middle school now."

"It's fine with me," I said, glancing at Eric. "What else do you guys have plann—"

I gasped. A thick vein pulsed out of Eric's rapidly reddening forehead, his eyes bulging as he clawed at his throat.

"Star! Call 9-1-1!"

I launched out of my seat, my body jolting into autopilot.

"Mom!"

"Stay clear, he's choking," I said. "I'm going to try and get it up."

I hauled Eric to his feet and wrapped my arms around his diaphragm from behind. I tried to remember the correct position of my hands and the upward pumping motion I needed to make. Luckily, it didn't take long for Eric to dislodge the chunk of pumpkin bread.

"WHORLOGUH!"

Hot, chunky bile gushed forth in a shockingly forceful stream all over my dining room table. Eric went limp in my arms. Star screamed.

———

"Is Dad gonna die?" Star sobbed quietly in the passenger seat as we drove home from the hospital. The sun was beginning to set and we were both tired and dirty and frazzled.

"No, they're going to take good care of him. He's had a lot of medicine, so the doctor thinks he'll rest for a while. Grandma Suzy says she'll text me when he wakes up."

"What happened?"

"They don't know," I said. "He abused his body for a long time, so when he gets sick, it really takes a toll. His blood pressure was through the roof, and that caused him to have a seizure."

"But why did he puke like that?" Star asked. "There was so much."

Right. The puke. I wasn't looking forward to the mess waiting for us at home.

"Well, I don't know. Maybe he ate too fast or something," I said. "Ugh."

"Do…do you think my pumpkin bread made him sick?" Star gazed at me with guilt in her eyes.

"No. I don't see how it could. We didn't get sick," I said. "It was probably just one of those things."

When Star and I returned home we were greeted with the most awful smell.

"Help me open some windows."

I held my breath, but the aroma of bile and stomach contents still stung my tastebuds. I grabbed a face mask as I set to the task of cleaning up my dining area. We had left in such a hurry to follow the ambulance to the hospital that I just left everything as it was. The plate of ruined pumpkin bread sat in the middle of the dining room table, splattered with chunky pools of yuck. I pulled out a pair of rubber gloves, a bucket, and a roll of paper towel and got to work.

As I cleaned, a core memory came unlocked from deep inside the vault of my mind. I was around nine or ten years old when I spilled an entire bowl of vegetable beef soup on my grandmother's carpet. Why people used to have carpets in their dining rooms I will never know. As my grandmother helped me clean up the mess, she told me about a dinner party that she had once.

"All six of my friends got sick all over the carpet. I had to rent a very expensive shampooer the next day to get it all out."

I glanced at the plate on the table. Grandma Maddie told me she had only used those plates one time—for a dinner party that went wrong. She never used them again. Maybe now I could understand why. When I was finished cleaning, I took the plate back to the closet and pulled out the entire box. The idea of eating off of the plates again made me nauseous.

I returned the plate to its box, closed the flap, and shut the closet door.

Chapter Fourteen

VERONICA

Eric was released from the hospital the following day. He was told to take a week off from work and start blood pressure medication, but otherwise, his lab results came back fine. I couldn't help but feel guilty about the whole situation. I felt responsible, as though I was the one who caused him to get sick. I was happy he was going to be okay, for Star's sake, at the very least. She had just gotten her dad back, and losing him now would be a truly devastating blow. Even though I didn't think much about my own non-existent father, I didn't want Star to be without hers.

The week flew by, and soon, it was time for my Saturday morning vending event. The Halloween Market in downtown Fort Myers is my favorite yearly event. Even though I don't get as many sales as some of my other vending events, it's still a festive and fun scene. Customers also remember me and come back to purchase holiday gifts at the Christmas market. Star brings a video game or a book to keep herself amused, and we usually spend the day chatting with other vendors, snacking on junk from food trucks, and enjoying the good weather. This year, however, fate stationed me near my business rival and sometimes nemesis, Billie.

Billie and I had gone to school together, though she was a few years younger than me. I didn't remember her from school, but a while back, I did start to notice her at many of the indie fairs and swap meets. She completely copied my entire business plan, from the name of her online store (Billie's Boutique) all the way down to her look and the wares that she sold. Her wife was a manager at one of the bigger thrift stores in town, so she was able to snag plenty of vintage items before they hit the sales floor, usually for free. I knew this because she bragged to me about it. I tried to let the situation roll off my back and ignore her, but like a hand-carved antique wooden boomerang, she always came back.

"Hi, Veronica."

I struggled to maintain a neutral expression as Bille approached my booth. Even the way she said my name was jarring. I gave Star a side-long glance as she read her paperback in the folding chair next to me. Star didn't care for Billie, either.

"Hi, Billie. How are sales today?"

"Great, actually. I scored some vintage Halloween decorations over the summer and was saving them for this event. People are snapping them up."

Billie snapped her fingers in the air in a z-motion, punctuating her words with a red-lipped smile.

"That's great, Billie." I forced a smile.

"Oooh! What are these?" She picked up one of my grandmother's plates I had displayed near my vintage kitchen wares. "Is this a complete set?"

"Yep. Full service. 1964, I believe, porcelain with Carolina blue glaze."

"How much do you want for them?"

"Well…" The idea of Billie getting my grandmother's plates made me feel hateful and possessive all at once. Sure, the plates creeped me out, but they were still special to me. Complete sets of identical plates had sold at auctions for over $400, but shipping fragile items was a nightmare. I preferred to sell my delicate items in person whenever possible, even if I had to do it at a discount rate.

"They're $300 on my online store, but I'll sell them to you for $250."

I sat back and exchanged a knowing glance with Star. Even my daughter knew the price was high for vintage plates, porcelain or not. The truth was, even though I didn't want the plates in the house anymore, I didn't exactly want Billie to have them either.

"Well, I did sell that vintage witch doll for $200 to that man from West Palm Beach," Billie said, admiring the plates. "What the heck. I'll take them."

My heart leaped in my throat. My instincts were to snap at her, yank the plate from her hands and tell her to fuck off, to quit copying me. But I couldn't lose my cool in front of a bunch of customers, especially not in front of Star. I swallowed my pride and nodded.

"Cash, card, or Venmo?"

"I'll Venmo you. I think I still have your info from when I bought all those dresses." Billie took out her phone and began to tap at the screen. "Do you know, I turned around and flipped them for like $100 each in my store? A-line dresses really had a moment there for a minute."

My face grew hot as I reached for the bubble wrap. My phone pinged, and a notification showed up.

You've got cash! Billie's Boutique has sent you $250.

Too late. It was a done deal.

"All set! Oh, you don't have to bother wrapping those up for me. I have a much better method to transport them." Billie grabbed the stack of plates and gave me a triumphant grin. "Happy early birthday to me! Enjoy the rest of your day!"

"You too." I gritted my teeth and forced a smile.

Star glared over the top of her book as Billie walked away with my grandmother's plates in her hand. We met each other's gaze at the same time with twin expressions of disgust.

I shook my head. "I really don't like her."

"Me neither," Star said. "I hope Grandma Millie's plates make her puke, too."

I should have been happy to make the sale, but I was too sad, too disappointed, too put off by the whole situation. I don't have the cornerstone on vintage resale, and there were plenty of others out there just like me, but I couldn't deny the fact that her blatant ripoff most likely contributed to my recent financial hardships, at least locally. Unfortunately, that is how the real world is. Dog eat dog, as they say.

I didn't have long to mull over the loss of my grandmother's plates to Billie before another visitor stopped by my booth. A tall shadow cast itself across my entire storefront as the silhouette of a man blocked out the midday sun. I recognized him immediately. Even though I had only met Dietzer once before, his striking features and imposing figure weren't easy to forget.

"Miss. Marquette, this is a nice surprise." Dietzer extended his hand across the counter. "What lovely wares you have."

"Mr. Dietzer, nice to see you again." I accepted his hand and shook it. His grip was firm and cold. "This is my daughter, Star."

Dietzer nodded. "I know it's been a while since we spoke, but I do hope that you've given my offer some thought."

I gave him a cautious smile, still reeling from this surprise visit. This guy sure liked to appear out of nowhere. "Thank you. It's a very generous offer, but I've decided not to sell."

"That's too bad. My interested party is very anxious to acquire this piece."

"Really? I'm surprised."

"Why is that?"

I paused. Dietzer wasn't showing me all of his cards. Antique dealers typically couldn't be trusted when it came to the value or authenticity of their wares. In this case, I had the piece he was trying to acquire, so the ball was in my court. But I wasn't exactly willing to show all of my cards either.

"Because the cabinet doesn't seem particularly interesting to me. I mean, it holds sentimental value for me, but it doesn't really strike me as a special piece."

Dietzer gave me a smile that made my skin crawl. "Oh, I assure you. It's very special. You see, it's crafted from a very desirable and rare wood. Do you know what the word *credenza* means?"

I shrugged. "I suppose I never really thought about it."

"It's an Italian word that means belief or trust. Do you have faith, Miss Marquette?"

"Faith in what?"

"In other beings. Other planes of existence. Spirits. The unexplained."

I glanced at Star. She was pretending to read her book, but I could tell her ears were perked at this particular conversation.

"Not really. I'm something of a realist, I suppose."

"Well, the man who commissioned the original version of this sideboard in the 1800s *did* believe in that sort of thing. He was a spiritualist, a holy man with a church of his own followers known as The Divinity. Back then, it was customary for holy men to have a table, called a *credenza,* in which their food was laid out like a buffet and tasted by their faithful followers to prevent poisoning. Those followers in The Divinity who were faithful enough to consume the poisoned food and live were thought to be blessed with eternal life."

"So, my grandmother's cabinet was intended to be a poison-tasting table for some weirdo church?"

"In essence, yes." Dietzer pulled a handkerchief from his pocket and dabbed his forehead. "So you see, this credenza of yours holds great historical value."

I blinked, trying to digest the information Dietzer had just laid out for me. While this wild explanation helped make sense of the price tag, little else about his story sounded right. Still, I was intrigued and couldn't help but want more answers.

"So, how did this historical piece of furniture end up in my grandmother's hands?"

"That's the million-dollar question, isn't it?" Dietzer threw me another serpentine grin. "My buyer seems to think that it was sent to America by mistake and was never intended to be sold."

"How strange."

He pulled out another business card. "If you should change your mind and want to sell, be sure to give me a call."

I took the business card again. The first card from Dietzer was still stuck to my fridge with a seashell magnet, staring me in the face every day. "Will do."

"Good day." Dietzer turned and disappeared into the crowd.

Before I could respond, a couple dressed in matching

Halloween T-shirts edged up to my booth and began to rummage through my crate of used vinyls. The woman held up a well-worn sleeve featuring a woman covered in whipped cream.

"How much for this Tijuana Brass?"

———

"That Dietzer guy was weird."

Star loaded up my hand cart with boxes of product as I finished wrapping up my canopy tent. The sun was low on the horizon, and the Halloween Market had dwindled down to just a few stray window shoppers. We had already broken down most of our table, and I was left with almost as much stock as I started with. Other than selling the plates to Billie and a handful of other knick-knacks, sales had been pretty low for the day.

"He's definitely a strange character," I said. "But at least I finally got some information on the credenza."

"Are you gonna sell it to him?" Star asked. "I mean, I'm not going to want to have it at my house someday. You might as well get some cash out of it now while you can."

"You mean you don't want to hold on to all of your mom's old junk when I die?" I gave her a playful nudge. "I guess you're right. Still, the whole situation is creepy."

"He said it was a poison table?"

"Not exactly. I guess it was a table designed so people could serve food to a holy man and make sure it wasn't poisoned."

"Sounds weird," Star said. "Maybe that's why Dad got sick."

"What do you mean?"

"Weren't Grandma's dishes stored in that cabinet a long time ago?"

"Yeah…"

"So maybe the cabinet made the dishes poisoned or something." Star shrugged. "Just a thought."

"Don't let his story put ideas into your head." I rolled my eyes. "He probably made it all up so he could get more of a commission from whoever wants to buy the cabinet."

"But what if it's true? What if there really is something weird about that cabinet, and it just keeps hurting people." Her voice grew thin as if her throat tightened.

I paused my work and turned to face Star.

My daughter was in tears.

"Hey, it's okay!" I pulled her into a hug. She buried her face into my shoulder, like she used to when she was little. The front of my dress was instantly soaked with warm tears. "I didn't realize it bothered you so much."

"I hate it!" Star said, her voice muffled into my chest. She pulled away and glanced up at me with shining eyes. "Sometimes…sometimes I think it's whispering to me."

The blood in my veins stilled. "What do you mean *whispering*?"

"It says things to me. It tries to get me to do things."

My thoughts turned to my mother. To myself. Great. All of us Marquette women really are nutjobs, and now it's rubbing off on Star. Well, not on my watch.

"That does it. When we get home, I'm going to call Dietzer and I'm going to sell it. I wish you would have told me this sooner."

"Do you believe me?"

I nodded. "Yeah. I've heard things, too. My mother has. I'll bet Grandma Maddie heard things but never would have admitted it."

Star's pinched expression relaxed, and her shoulders softened. Her entire body seemed to sigh with relief.

"Thanks, Mom. Thank you for believing me."

"I'll always believe you."

I hugged Star again, and this time, my throat closed up. I didn't want to fall apart in front of her. I swallowed the lump in my throat and let out a laugh instead. "So, we should go on a vacation after we sell that thing, huh?"

"Really?" Star laughed and wiped at her eyes.

"Yeah, where do you wanna go? Paris? Japan? We'll have to get passports, but…"

"Antarctica."

"Really?" I laughed. "But it's so cold!"

The rest of the way home, Star and I joked and laughed about what we should do with ten thousand dollars. We decided we should save some of it, of course, then go on a big summer vacation to Europe. We had such a good time dreaming about the possibilities a sudden windfall could hold that I didn't even notice right away that my front door was open when we pulled into the driveway.

"Star, don't forget to bring in that box with the vinyl records. We can leave the rest until tomorrow—"

"Mom. Someone is in our house."

For the second time that day, I froze. All feeling left my body as I watched a figure glide across my living room through my front picture window.

A figure with an ax held high.

Chapter Fifteen

VERONICA

I STARED in disbelief as my mother hacked away at the credenza. I didn't bother trying to stop her, only watching in horror from afar as I spoke with the emergency dispatcher in hushed tones. Star and I waited in the car with the engine running and ready to go if my mother decided to bolt out the front door. In the dim dining room light, we saw her sink the ax into the credenza again and again, causing chunks of walnut to fly all around her like some kind of demented wood chipper.

It didn't take long for red and blue flashing lights to illuminate my driveway. A half-dozen men dressed in military-grade black uniforms surrounded my home with guns held high. Everything happened so fast, and before I knew it, the police had subdued my mother and brought her out of the house in handcuffs. She made eye contact with me for a moment as she was shoved into the back of a cruiser, her expression twisted and half-crazed.

"You're safe now!" She yelled in my direction. "I love you!"

A tremor ran down my body as I clutched Star to my chest. I wanted to press her into me, wrap her body up tight, and shield her from all of this. Her life wasn't supposed to go this way. She wasn't supposed to see and hear the things I had to see. She wasn't supposed to hurt. We sat there and sobbed until a face I recognized approached. Star and I exited the vehicle as I tried to regain my composure.

"Officer Kincaid. Thank you for coming." I sniffed and wiped at my face. "Is my mother okay?"

"She's unharmed. She won't see the outside for a while, though. She didn't comply when told to put down her weapon."

"I'm so sorry." I placed a hand on my mouth and stifled a sob.

Star wrapped her arms around my waist.

We held onto each other as we answered more of the officer's questions. *No, we didn't go into the house. No, I don't know how she got in. No, we didn't know why she would be there. No, we didn't get hurt.*

I swayed on my feet, dazed as nosy neighbors stood on the street to watch, all of them taking in the action and none of them offering to help. I was among a sea of people and all of them were strangers, living among a community but not actually in it.

I watched the police go in and out of my home,

talking amongst themselves. One by one, they got into their cruisers, leaving just Office Kincaid to speak with me. Soon, Star and I would be alone again, left to deal with the aftermath. I didn't know if I was strong enough to go back in there and face what my mother had done. She broke into my home, destroyed something that was important and valuable. Any hope of reconciling with her was lost.

"Do you have anyone you can talk to? Professionally?"

I glanced up at Officer Kincaid and shook my head. "Not really."

"I would call someone. A counselor or a professional," she said, glancing at Star. "For you both. This kind of trauma isn't always easy to digest."

"What kind of trauma?"

Officer Kincaid blinked, but her expression remained neutral. "Domestic abuse. Mental health issues."

Officer Kincaid gave me her business card again with the case number written on it. She tipped her hat and offered me a sympathetic smile. "I'm just a call away if anything else happens."

"Thanks."

I glanced at the business card as Officer Kincaid began to walk away. "Hey, are we allowed to go back in there?"

The officer turned back to face me. "Yeah, you're free to go in there."

"Isn't it a crime scene? Don't they need to take pictures or something?"

Officer Kincaid gave me a sideways look and shook her head. "No. Nothing was disturbed."

Star and I exchanged glances.

"You all have a good night." Before I could ask any more questions, Officer Kincaid slid behind the wheel of her cruiser and pulled away.

Star tugged at my sleeve. "Can we stay at a hotel tonight?"

I nodded. "Yeah. I just need to get the credit card out of the freezer and lock the house up. Not that it matters, I guess."

"Can I come with?"

"No, just wait here. I'll be quick."

I walked toward my front door on shaky knees, preparing myself for an alarming sight. I couldn't understand why Officer Kincaid had said nothing had been disturbed. I saw my mother hack the credenza to pieces with my own eyes. However, as I crossed the threshold into my living room, I realized the only thing amiss was my living room rug and a few dining room chairs.

The credenza was still intact, staring back at me—a single, solid, shining, wooden piece.

———

"Two cheeseburgers with fries, please? Yes, with ketchup. Oh, and a can of rootbeer and do you have a full liquor bar? Great, I'll take two vodkas and a can of cranberry juice. Thanks."

Star was settled into the middle of her own giant,

fluffy, king-sized bed. Her hair was wrapped in a towel, and she wore the swanky embroidered robe that came with our beachfront hotel room. In a bag on the dresser were two sets of brightly colored clothes and toiletries for each of us, last-minute supplies acquired at the hotel's gift shop. The next bill on my credit card was going to be enormous, but it would be worth it after the night we had.

"How ya hanging in there, kiddo?" I sat on the bed next to Star and sunk into the mattress. I wanted to let it envelop me, fold me in layers of soft, white comfort. But I needed a shower and some comfort food first.

"I'm okay."

"It's okay if you're not, though," I said. "I'm going to call around tomorrow to see if we can talk to someone. You know, a counselor. About what happened."

"I don't get it," Star said. "Why did the cops say nothing was disturbed? We saw Grandma chopping up the cabinet."

I pursed my lips. "I don't know. I can't explain it either."

"But it was like nothing ever happened!" Star sat up in bed, her eyes wild.

I had tried to keep her from seeing it, but there was no point in hiding anything. We both watched as my mother destroyed the credenza. We both saw the shards of wood fly in the air and heard the crazed hacking noises coming from inside our dining room. To say that we were shocked to find the cabinet completely unharmed and undisturbed would be an understatement.

"Well, we are going to stay right here on the beach until I sell the credenza to Dietzer," I said. "I'll hire movers and deliver it myself if I have to. I've had enough."

"I just don't understand. Why is this happening?"

"I don't know," I said. "I can't explain it either."

"Maybe Grandma isn't crazy," Star said. "Maybe the cabinet really is cursed. She said she was trying to protect us."

I sighed. "I know. I never used to believe in that kind of thing. Now, I'm not so sure."

"And what about the gross book we tried to burn?" Star said. "Just because you don't believe something doesn't mean it's not true."

She had me there. "I guess you're right."

Star slumped back into her pillow. "What's going to happen to Grandma now?"

"I don't know. She resisted arrest and threatened those officers, so she might be in jail for a long time."

"I feel bad for her," Star said.

"Me too."

My throat was dry. *Where is room service anyway?*

I walked to the glass sliding door and stood out on the balcony to take in some fresh air. It was a windy autumn evening, and the stars were in their full glory over the Gulf of Mexico. I breathed in a deep lungful of salty air and closed my eyes, listening to the gentle *rahh, rahh, rahh* of the crashing waves.

I opened my eyes and scanned the dark shoreline. In the distance, a figure walked along the shore in slow, graceful movements. Her white puff of hair stood out under the moonlight, and her pink and white lace pajamas rustled in the breeze. I watched as my grandmother walked into the ocean and let the waves take her out to sea.

Knock, knock, knock.

I turned my head toward the door as a muffled male voice floated through the breeze. "Room service."

I blinked and glanced back at the empty shoreline. I was seeing things again.

I retrieved our room service order, my stomach rumbling at the smell of too much grease and too much salt. Star and I sat and ate our dinner on the bed in silence, both of us staring at the sitcom on TV, but neither of us laughing. When dinner was finished, I took a shower and changed into the oversized Fort Myers Beach tie-dyed T-shirt I bought at the gift shop. I poured myself a double vodka with a splash of cranberry juice and slipped into bed. Star was still wide awake.

"Have you talked to your dad yet?" I asked.

Star nodded. "Yeah. I called him when you were in the shower."

"What did he have to say?"

"He said I could stay with him and Grandma Suzy if I needed to," Star said, scrolling through her phone.

A pang of envy stabbed my heart. "Oh? What do you think about that?"

Star shrugged. "I don't know. I still have school and stuff. Her house is like, two hours away."

"Well, you can go if you don't feel safe…"

"Mom. I'm not going to leave you," Star said. "I think once that cabinet is out of the house, we'll both feel better."

"Yeah. Me too."

I laid back on the pillow, my eyes suddenly very heavy. Nervous energy shuddered through my body as I pulled the thick down coverlet over me. There was much to do, much to think about and consider, and I didn't have the energy needed to face any of it anymore.

Chapter Sixteen

KAREN, 1984

KAREN MARQUETTE HAD JUST GOTTEN home from her morning shift at the grocery store on that fateful afternoon in November. It had been a busy, exhausting day, with more customers than usual stocking up on frozen turkeys, freeze-dried mashed potatoes, and canned corn for the upcoming holiday. She had laid out a blanket for baby Veronica in the living room with some toys and put on Sesame Street to keep her entertained. She had only meant to rest her eyes. She didn't mean to fall asleep.

Karen woke to her two-year-old daughter standing over her, her face covered in blood.

"Mama, go boom."

Veronica slapped the side of her face with an open, chubby palm.

"Boom, boom, boom!"

Fine droplets of blood smattered across Karen's face as Veronica's sleepy gaze zeroed in on her hands. There was blood. *So much blood.* Her baby's hand was covered in red like some kind of messy finger painting experiment gone wrong. The streaks of gore seemed strange and out of place against her perfect dark curls, her soft, rosy cheeks, and rainbow-print jumper. A sizable gash oozed blood on her brow, the wound dangerously close to her eye.

"Oh, baby! What happened?"

A low whine escaped from Veronica's little mouth as she realized there was blood on her hand. *Her* blood. She reached up to touch the wound on her face, and the low whine turned up to a wail.

Madeline Marquette rushed into the room, a dish towel in her hands. "What's going on?"

"I don't know!" Karen said. "I just laid down for a minute and then the next thing I knew, she was screaming."

"How could you be so careless?" Madeline scooped the wailing Veronica up and carried her to the kitchen.

Karen followed, surveying the scene. The lamp that normally sat on the side table was on the ground near the credenza, the cord unplugged from the wall in a tangle.

"Let me see." Madeline sat Veronica on the kitchen countertop and ran the water in the sink. "This might need stitches."

"Mom, I think she hit her head on the cabinet," Karen said.

"Get me some paper towels. We need to clean this baby up," Madeline said. "Oh, you poor little girl."

"Mom, did you hear me?" Karen said, passing her a wad of paper towels. "It's that damn cabinet!"

"I heard you. We need to take care of this wound first," Madeline said, making soft shushing sounds as she dabbed at the wound.

Veronica continued to wail.

"There, there. It's not so bad."

"I knew it. I knew it!" Karen paced back and forth across the yellow linoleum flooring. "That cabinet—it's dangerous!"

"Karen, please calm down…"

"No! You've never believed me!" Karen grabbed her head and doubled over.

Veronica wailed louder.

"You're scaring the baby!" Madeline said, bundling Veronica up. "I'm taking her to the pediatrician. It won't stop bleeding."

"What's going on, Ma?" Mike Marquette appeared in the kitchen doorway, still dressed in his grease-streaked work shirt from the mechanic's shop. His eyes grew wide as he took in the sight of his niece covered in blood. "Holy cow, what happened?"

"Veronica had a little accident," Madeline said over Veronica's cries. "Help your sister—she's out of control again."

"No one ever listens to me!" Karen sobbed, her entire body shaking.

Mike grabbed Karen around the shoulders and held her tight. "Hey, it's okay."

Thick globs of snot ran down Karen's face as she

sobbed, trapped in her brother's restrictive embrace. "Don't let her take my baby away!"

"She's just taking her to the doctor," Mike said, his grip still tight as a vice. "Karen, please. You gotta calm down!"

"We're all gonna die!" Karen sobbed. "We're all gonna die!"

Chapter Seventeen

VERONICA

"Uncle Mike, it's me. Veronica."

"Ronnie! How's it going?"

I sat on the patio with my cup of coffee the following morning, overlooking a breathtaking view of the Gulf of Mexico. It was a crisp Sunday in late October, and I should have been happy. Relaxed. At ease. Instead, I had difficult phone calls to make. I needed answers. And I needed help.

"Not so good," I said. "Mom broke into my house last night and was arrested."

"Oh no." My uncle cleared his throat, and the receiver crackled in my ear as if he were shifting position. "Well, I didn't give her your address."

"It's okay. I'm not unlisted or anything. I suppose she could have found me any time," I said. "It was really scary though."

"She didn't try to hurt you or Star, did she?"

"Not exactly." I paused. *How do I explain what happened?* There was no use telling my version of the truth. Best to keep things simple. "She tried to chop Gran's cabinet up with an ax, though."

"Not again." Uncle Mike let out an exasperated sigh.

"What do you mean, not again?"

"I had to hold her back from tearing that cabinet apart more than once. She was always fixated on that dang thing."

"Did…do you know if Gran ever tried to get mom help? Like, a therapist or anything?"

"Well, only rich folks did that sort of thing back then," he said. "Right about the time she was pregnant with you, your grandma tried to take her to church for counseling with the pastor, but that never lasted."

"When she was pregnant?"

"Yeah, that was a pretty awful time. Whenever Mom would try to grill Karen about who your father was, she would either clam up or start screamin'." Uncle Mike paused, his breathing heavy on the line. "It was awful. None of us could figure out how to help her. But then you were born, and she loved you so much. She straightened out for a while after that."

My heart squeezed in my chest. Talking about my early years was never easy for our family, especially when it came to the subject of my absent father. Uncle Mike had never been one much to share his feelings, either. Perhaps he had softened a bit after Grandma Maddie's passing.

"Do you think you could come down here and help

with some things? I know you were just here for Gran's funeral, but I could really use the support."

"What kind of things?"

"I don't know. Legal stuff with Mom. Maybe we can get her some mental health help. She's always resisted whenever I talk about it, but this time, I think we have to insist."

"I wish I could come, kiddo. I've got a big job coming into the Chicago office next week, and I need to be here to oversee it."

"That's okay. What about Uncle Jimmy?"

"He's off on some hiking expedition in South America, I think. Trying to go find himself, or whatever."

"Okay." My face grew hot. I was going to have to deal with this alone. Again. "Before I let you go, can you tell me anything you remember about Mom and why she's so obsessed with the cabinet? Anything from when you were younger?"

"I remember when you smacked your face against it," he said, letting out a low whistle. "She lost her mind after that happened. I didn't know so much blood could come out of a little person."

"I know about that, but what else?"

Uncle Mike sighed. "Well, she said the voices told her the wood from the cabinet was special."

"Voices?"

"Yeah, you know she heard all sorts of things. Crazy stuff."

"Can you try and remember? Please. It's important." I glanced over my shoulder. Star was probably listening to everything I said. I lowered my voice. "I'm going to get counseling for Star and me. If there's any kind of family mental health history I can provide… I don't know. There's so much I don't know about our family history. No one ever talked about it. I just need some answers so I can make sure Star and I are okay."

Uncle Mike sighed into the receiver. In the background, I could hear the clanking of metal and the whine of brakes. He was probably itching to get back to work.

"Well, from what I remember, she said that the voices who talked to her…" He took a heavy pause and lowered his voice. "She said the voices told her she was descended from a line of witches. That it was her job to protect you."

"Witches."

"Mhmm. Toldya she was nuts. She said these witches were caretakers of the wood and had to make sure that no one ever got hold of it, or bad things would happen. She said the wood was cursed. Evil."

"Where would she get an idea like that?"

"I don't know. After your dad left, she started doing and saying all sorts of crazy things. I think it was the drugs."

The springs on Star's bed creaked as she got up and walked to the bathroom. Time to end the conversation. Uncle Mike wasn't going to be much help anyway.

"Okay, well, I gotta go."

"Take care of yourself, Ronnie."

"I always do."

I hung up feeling worse and with even more questions than before. It was the weekend, so I knew trying to make a counseling appointment would have to wait. But there was another call I could make in the meantime. I grabbed my purse from the counter, fished out Dietzer's business card, and punched his number into my phone.

It only rang once.

"Hello?"

"Dietzer. It's Veronica Marquette. I'm calling about—"

"The credenza. Yes. Lovely to hear from you, Miss Marquette."

"I'm calling because I'm finally ready to part with my grandmother's cabinet if your buyer is still interested."

"Oh, they are indeed still interested," Dietzer said. I could practically hear his lips stretching into a joker-like grin on the other side. "When will be a good time to come and pick it up?"

———

Star and I lounged around that morning, eating pancakes and bacon from the room service menu and enjoying the beach. A weight seemed to lift from both our shoulders when I told her Dietzer would be picking up the credenza the following day. It was nearly Halloween, a time of year we usually enjoyed. Unfortunately, the real terrors in our life this year had been making it difficult for us to enjoy tricks or treats of any kind.

We walked along the shore later that day under the haze of an early autumn sky. Hurricane season was over, but cottony cloud streaks along the horizon hinted that another storm was coming. For now, the bathtub-warm green water of the gulf lapped calmly along the shore in frothy, gentle waves. Most folks enjoyed the beach best during the peak of summer, but this time of year was when I liked being near the coast best.

"So what happens next?" Star picked up a purple coquina and held the butterfly-shaped shell up to the sky to examine it in the sunlight.

"Well, I was thinking we'll stay here another night, and I'll drop you off at school tomorrow morning. When you get home, we'll be $10,000 richer, and the credenza will be gone."

"What about Halloween?"

"What about it?"

"Kayla wanted us to go trick-or-treating."

"Do you still want to go?"

Star shrugged. "I guess."

I breathed in deeply, gazing out toward the horizon. I mulled over the disturbing new information my uncle had laid out for me and realized that I needed mental and emotional help more than ever. *Did I really see Grandma Maddie's ghost last night?* Or at the library, or in my home? Or was I just imagining that I was seeing her because I was lonely and grieving? Was I creating all this drama to distract me from the real-life stuff I had to deal with? I had read once about how people can suffer from decision fatigue, and something as simple as figuring out what to make for dinner can cause them to shut down. I could relate. I was tired of doing it all on my own. I was tired of having to be the one with all the answers all the time. I wanted to walk out into the sea and follow my grandmother's spirit, let the waves consume me. But I couldn't, and I wouldn't. As long as I had Star to look out for, I had to keep going.

"I heard you talking to Uncle Mike," Star said, tossing the coquina back into the sea.

I nodded. "Yeah. I was hoping he could help me with some stuff."

"What were you talking about witches for?"

I frowned. "Well, your Uncle Mike was just giving me some information. I was trying to find out about some of the things my mom used to say. You know, certain mental health issues can be hereditary. I want to make sure if we have any of the same symptoms, our health care provider will know about it."

"I hear them, too."

My feet came to a halt in the wet sand. I resisted the urge to doubt her, to push aside what she was saying. Isn't that what everyone did to my mother? Hadn't I heard voices myself?

"When do you hear them?" I asked her.

"Only when I'm at home," Star said. "They scare me."

"What do you do when you hear them?" My heart began to beat fast.

"I just put in my earbuds and crank up some loud music," Star said. "It seems to help for a while."

Another beat passed between us. A vision of my mother turning the credenza into mulch flashed before my eyes. Star met my gaze and seemed to know exactly what I was thinking.

"The voices say the wood the cabinet is made from is special," Star said. "Do you think that's why Grandma couldn't destroy it?"

I took another deep breath, my lungs tight with anxiety. "I don't know. It's not going to be our problem for much longer, though. Once we get rid of the cabinet and talk to a therapist or a counselor or whatever, I think things are going to get better."

"What if it doesn't, though? What if things just keep getting worse?"

There it was. Star said the quiet part out loud. It was the same sentiment I had been thinking, but I didn't want to admit it. Didn't want to face it. What if getting rid of the credenza and talking to a counselor didn't do a damn thing? *What then?*

"Then we keep on fighting," I said, wrapping my arms around her shoulders. "We've come this far. I'm not about to give up yet."

Chapter Eighteen

VERONICA

THE FOLLOWING MORNING, Dietzer's van and moving crew were ready and waiting in my driveway when I returned home. I had already dropped Star off at school and was still dressed in a colorful beach dress from the hotel gift shop. An unusually cold October breeze wafted through the front yard, cutting through the lightweight cloth. I shivered and hugged my arms as I exited my car to greet the movers.

Four men wearing head-to-toe white biohazard suits flanked Dietzer on either side as another gust of chilly wind shook the white gauze ghosts hanging from my tree. The presence of Dietzer and his crew made for a dramatic scene, especially next to my six-foot-tall skeleton and animatronic werewolf decorations. My neighbor across the street stared at the house as I closed the car door, a newspaper in one hand and a sour expression on his lips. He was a retired man who hadn't bothered to say a word or even wave to Star or me the entire time we lived in the neighborhood.

I scowled and threw up my middle finger at him. "Getting a good enough look?"

The man grumbled and turned back toward his house. For a brief moment, I felt a sense of triumph. But when I glanced back at the driveway, my gut sank again.

"Good morning, Miss Marquette." Dietzer approached me with a hand extended. I accepted his reach and shook it. "That's a…very lovely color on you."

"Thanks. We were at the beach." I nodded toward his moving crew. "What's with the hazmat suits?"

"Oh, you can never be too careful moving things," Dietzer said. "Dust, pet dander, all the pathogens floating around these days with viruses and whatnot. We just like to ensure that our people are safe."

"Okay." I frowned, trying not to glare. "It's this way."

I unlocked the front door and let the crew of men in, each of them taller and heavier than me. The credenza was heavy, but Star and I had managed to move it without too much difficulty. Four movers seemed to be overkill. Even though it was broad daylight, I was suddenly overcome with the realization that I once again invited unknown men into my home. Men who wouldn't leave a trace of biological evidence in my home if they killed me then and there. My fight or flight instinct kicked in, and I walked back out the front door as fast as my adrenaline-numbed legs would take me.

Dietzer was waiting for me just outside the threshold

to my home, his rictus grin spread wide and a thick, white bank envelope in his hand.

"I hope you don't mind cash for this transaction," he said, handing me the envelope. "My buyer wanted the transaction to be smooth and painless. Cutting a large check would have been more complicated, you see."

I took the envelope, opened the flap, and thumbed through the stack of hundred dollar bills. A quick assessment told me it was all there; if not, close enough. I wanted this to be over. I shoved the stack back into the envelope and stuck it in my purse.

"Cash is fine," I said. "Thanks again for being patient while I made my decision."

"No worries at all. I know how sentimental family heirlooms can be."

Footsteps fell behind me, and I turned to see the side of the credenza floating at face-level in my darkened doorway. The movers took turns easing their respective corners of the cabinet out of the house one by one, taking care not to bump the door frame.

"Careful now. Mind the finish."

Dietzer waved the crew over to the delivery van and opened the back doors. He directed as they eased the credenza into the back. When the credenza was safely inside, the men entered the van and shut the door behind them.

"Well, that just about does it." Dietzer returned to where I was standing and pulled a purple flier from his pocket. "Before I leave, I want to invite you to one of our meetings. I belong to an association for antique dealers, and well, I figured you might be interested in joining, what with your little business and all."

Little business. I scoffed and took the flier. It wasn't the first time I had someone look down their elitist nose at me. If he hadn't just paid me a wad of cash, I would have politely told him to fuck right off.

"Thank you, Dietzer. I'll look into it."

"Good day, Miss Marquette."

I waited and watched as the moving van pulled out of my driveway, taking the credenza and hopefully all of my worries away with it. The stack of bills sat in my purse like a stone. I needed to take this stack of cash to the bank and fast. I crumbled up the purple flier without looking at it, locked the front door of my home, and got back into the car.

I had a cash deposit to make.

———

"Boo!"

I let out a pretend squeal of terror as a little girl dressed as a witch appeared at my front door.

"Twick or tweet!"

She smiled up at me with a milk-toothed grin, no older than four or five. Her costume was elaborate and clearly homemade, with velvet and lace finishes you wouldn't typically find on a child's costume. She held out a black cauldron candy bucket and gazed up at me expectantly.

"Well, you're a pretty little witch," I said, dropping a

packet of M&Ms into her bucket. I glanced up at the woman behind her, likely her mother. "Your costume is amazing."

"I'm not pretty—I'm scary!" the little girl said.

I let out a laugh. "It's okay. You can be both."

"Sorry, she's had a lot of sugar already," the mom said, her cheeks flushed with embarrassment.

"Don't worry about it. Happy Halloween!"

"Happy Halloween!" The mother-daughter duo joined hands and disappeared back into the night.

Trick-or-Treat was winding down, and so was my energy. Our neighborhood seemed to have fewer families with small children every year. Everyone was growing up, including my daughter. She sat on the couch, scrolling on her phone and eating the spoils she had collected with her friends as Bette Midler broke into a witchy cabaret act on the TV screen.

"Are you going to watch TV or your phone?" I teased and sank into the couch next to her.

"Both." Star held her candy bucket towards me.

I plucked out an Almond Joy and unwrapped it. "How was trick-or-treating?"

"Fine."

"Just fine?"

Star shrugged. "Our neighborhood is kinda dead."

"Yeah. It's certainly not as fun as it used to be." I sighed as the witch sisters danced on TV. "Well, I think I'm gonna call it a night."

"*Mom.*"

The tone in Star's voice was urgent. The sugary

chocolate and coconut mixture of the candy burned on my tongue as she turned her phone to face me.

"Isn't this the lady you sold Gran's plates to?"

I blinked and took Star's phone. Billie's red lips smiled back at me from the social media post Star had found during her scrolling. It wasn't her face that made me want to retch up the Halloween candy I had just consumed, but the headline underneath.

Local small-business owner found dead. Foul play suspected.

"The post said she died on her birthday," Star said, snatching her phone back from my hands. She scrolled to the social media page for Billie's Boutique. I was still blown away by how identical her layout and presentation were to my branding, right down to the font she used and the color scheme. I quickly shook away my irritation at her copycat antics. The woman was dead for crying out loud.

"Look." Star opened up another photo, one Billie had only posted the day before. It was a picture of Billie dressed in full pin-up attire in her retro-inspired kitchen. She had baked a pink and white cake with the caption, *"HBD to me!"* and a cake emoji.

"Okay, what am I…"

"No! *Look.*" Star pinched the screen and flicked to expand the photo. She didn't even have to say it out loud. I already knew.

"She displayed her birthday cake on Grandma Maddie's plates."

· · ·

It was Halloween night when Karen Marquette strapped her three-year-old daughter into the passenger side of her mother's Pontiac and tossed all her worldly belongings in the trunk. Little Veronica was dressed as a witch, the McCall's patterned gown barely covering her knees. Karen wasn't much of a seamstress, but she had found an adorable fabric pattern with spiders and candy corn all over it and wanted to give hand-made costumes a try. That's what a good mother would do, right? Well, like usual, Karen fucked it up and made the costume too small. Veronica didn't seem to notice or care, though.

"You stay here, punkin'," Karen said, closing the car door. "Mama needs to take care of something, and then I'll be right back."

She had to move fast if she was going to carry out her plan. It was a rare moment when she had the house all to herself. Mike and Jimmy were out at a Halloween party, and her mother had joined a new bridge club. This was her chance to finally make the voices stop. They told her exactly what she needed to do; they'd been telling her for years. She just had to find the courage to do it.

Inside, the house was dark and quiet. Karen had tried to move the credenza before, but it was too heavy. Stubborn. Even if she could move it on her own, she didn't have much time. It was a shame that the rest of the house would have to be destroyed with it, but it was a price she was willing to pay. No one was home, everyone would be safe, and she could finally send that goddamn piece of furniture back to whatever version of hell it came from.

Karen opened the third drawer and popped out the

false bottom. The disgusting green book and dagger were there, as they always were, staring back at her expectantly. She needed to make sure they were destroyed, too. She closed the drawer, dug a lighter out of her pocket, and turned toward the kitchen to grab the half-empty bottle of vodka from the cupboard.

It must be cleansed with fire, the voices said one last time, for good measure.

"I know," Karen said.

She glanced around the house, fear and regret threatening to take hold. Could she really do it? Could she really torch the credenza and her family home with it? She didn't see any other way.

Karen unscrewed the cap and splashed the credenza with vodka, soaking the top of the wood until the bottle was empty. On top of the cabinet were framed family photos, including one of just her mother and Veronica. She picked up the photo, and her throat tightened.

"I'm sorry."

Karen flicked the lighter, and an orange glow illuminated the dining room. The voices in her head grew louder, hissing.

Finish the job!

Do it!

What are you waiting for?

Their threats became more and more insistent, terrifying pleas as she stared into the flame. All she had to do was lower the lighter to the credenza, and it would all be over.

They're coming!

"Not this bullshit again."

A pair of strong arms wrapped around her shoulders. The lighter was snatched away from her hands.

"Karen, what the hell are you doing?"

Her brother, Jimmy, flicked on the dining room light. "Is that vodka?"

She struggled against Mike's firm grip. "No!"

"Karen, are you insane?" Mike squeezed her tighter. "Where's Veronica?"

"We have to burn it! Please, you don't understand…"

"Jimmy, go look for the baby. This has to end now," Mike shouted, his voice gruff in her ear. "Goddammit, where's Veronica?"

"She's safe! I would never hurt her! I would never hurt you," Karen whined, useless against his vice grip. Her body went slack. "I just wanted to make it stop."

"What's going on here?" Madeline walked through the front door, her eyes wide. "Michael, what's happening?"

"This psycho was gonna burn down the house," he said. "We need to call the cops and lock her up. This time, she's gone too far."

"Where's Veronica?" Madeline cried. "Where's my granddaughter?"

"I see her," Jimmy said. "She's in the car."

The voices in Karen's head stopped, and her thoughts cleared like clouds parting from the sun. They were going to take her daughter away. She knew it deep in her bones. She couldn't let that happen.

"No!" Karen snaked an arm free from her brother's

grip. She landed a swift elbow jab to his ribs. Mike let out a yowl as she wiggled away and sprinted toward the front door. She just needed to get to her daughter, get them away as far as they could go.

But again, she was too late.

"You're not taking her anywhere." Karen's mother stood next to the car with Veronica in her arms. Her daughter was crying.

"Come on, baby," Karen said, reaching for her. "Come with Mama."

Veronica buried her face into her grandmother's neck.

"She's scared of you," Madeline said. "You're no longer welcome in this house."

"I'm not leaving without her!"

"Ma, you want me to call the cops?" Mike stood in the doorway and placed a hand on his ribs.

Madeline shook her head. "Get your head right, Karen. Come back when you're ready to be a parent."

"But I…"

"I said no!"

Veronica began to wail.

Karen watched as her mother disappeared with her daughter into the house. Her brothers stood like two sentinels, barring her entry back into the place she grew up in. The only place she had ever called home. Karen got behind the wheel, backed out of the driveway, and drove off into the night.

Chapter Nineteen

VERONICA

"Do you think we accidentally killed that Billie lady?"

Red spray exploded from out of my nostrils onto the tabletop. Star was sitting across from me in a booth, picking at a soggy piece of salad. I quickly grabbed a napkin and dabbed at my nose, my sinuses burning from the house wine. Damn. What a waste.

"Why would you think that?"

"*Mom.*" Star glared at me under heavy brows. "That lady ate her birthday cake off Grandma's cursed plates."

"We don't know that," I said. "It's sad that she died, but…it has to be a coincidence, right?"

Star forked a bite of lasagna into her mouth. *"Donen soun like a coinciden ta me."*

"They don't know that's what killed her," I said. "Correlation does not imply causation."

"What does that mean?"

"It's a fancy way of saying that just because something looks like it was the cause doesn't mean that it really was. So just because you forgot to wash your hands doesn't mean that's why you got a cold."

"I see. So, like, don't always believe everything you see?"

"Something like that," I said. "Or don't assume you know everything until you have all the evidence."

"Right." Star rolled her eyes.

"Don't roll your eyes at me!" I hissed, lowering my voice. "I've struggled my entire life worrying that I would end up crazy just like my mother. I'm glad that you can take all of this at face value, but I can't."

"Mom," Star said. "You're not crazy."

I shifted in my seat. "I might be. But if I'm not crazy, and all of this—*stuff*—that's been happening is true? I don't know. I think I'm just scared to admit what it all might mean."

It was the first day of November, and we were enjoying a celebratory dinner at her favorite restaurant. I was nibbling on my third breadstick and halfway through my second glass of wine, desperate to consume as many comfort calories as I could. My savings account now boasted a balance with many lovely zeros in it, and the credenza was finally out of our hair, but I still felt a sense of unease. As Star had predicted, all was still not right with the world. I tried not to dwell on the lingering dread as I finished my wine and dug into my eggplant parmesan. The restaurant really wasn't so bad after all.

"Okay, so that Billie lady dying was just a coincidence," Star said. "But what about Grandma Karen?"

"What about her?"

"Come on. We're supposed to be honest with each other, right? We both saw what happened. The ax. The flying chunks of wood. We're just supposed to pretend that didn't happen, right?"

"I don't know how to explain it," I said. "I'm honestly scared to talk about it."

"Why?"

"No one believes when things like that happen," I said. "If I tell that story to a therapist or someone, what do you think will happen?"

"I don't know."

"Well, I have a good idea, and it's not pretty."

"So what do we do then? Pretend like it never happened?"

I shrugged. "I don't know a better way."

Star sighed and pushed her spaghetti off her plate. So much for a celebratory dinner.

"Well, we've got some extra cash at least," I said. "Now we can start really planning a kick-ass summer vacation. Where to first? London? Or Paris?"

"I don't know. I have to talk to Dad," Star said. She put down her fork and her expression pinched. "There's actually something I wanted to talk to you about."

"What?"

"Dad wanted to tell you himself before he ended up in the hospital. I told him I didn't think it was right to wait to tell you."

"Tell me what?"

"His job hired him full-time. He's going to move back here."

"Oh. Well, that's… That's nice. You'll be able to see him more then."

"He says he's going to get an apartment big enough for me to have a room there," she continued. "He asked if I would want to stay with him."

Heat bloomed at my cheeks as tears sprung up at the corners of my eyes. *Goddammit, Eric.*

"Is that something you want to do?" I asked her.

"Not really," she said.

Relief. I took a sip of water, trying to remain neutral. Star knew me too well anyway, but I didn't want her to make decisions like that based on my emotions alone.

"Well, if you ever change your mind, then that's okay too."

Star reached across the table and squeezed my hand. "I know, Mom."

———

The first week of November passed in a blur of estate sales, invoices, and trips to the post office. Folks were gearing up for the holiday season, which led to me making multiple sales per day and my little shop doing well. One of the fur coats I had refurbished even sold and I was relieved to be able to pre-pay the mortgage on the house for not only December but for January as well.

I kept the little nest egg of money from selling the credenza in my savings account and gazed at the balance often, dreaming about the European vacation Star and I would take next summer. I tried to look toward the future without fear. It wasn't so easy with the past always breathing down my neck.

"Hey, got a minute?"

It was Friday evening, and Eric was dropping off Star after their standing father/daughter dinner and movie date. I turned from my desk to see him standing in the doorway as Star rushed past me to her room. I exhaled and closed my eyes, preparing myself for what I was sure would be a difficult talk.

"Yeah, come on in."

I got up and moved to the dining room. I took a seat at the head of the table and Eric took a seat opposite of me. The last time we faced each other like this, I ended up performing the Heimlich and cleaning up puddles of puke.

"How are you feeling, by the way?" I asked.

Eric chuckled and leaned back in his chair. "Fine. I guess I should be grateful I choked. I had been feeling off for a while, and I just brushed it off. I didn't know I had high blood pressure. I gotta take pills for it now, but I'm feeling better."

"I'm glad to hear that."

"Did Star tell you I was offered a permanent position here?"

I nodded and picked at my nails. "She mentioned

that. Said you would even have a room for her if she needed it."

"Mhmm. I just thought, you know. It might take some of the burden off…"

"The *burden*?" My face flamed. "Our daughter isn't a *burden*."

"No! Of course, I didn't mean that, but…"

Lava erupted beneath my skin as all the synapses in my brain flashed. Something inside of me was snapping, something I had been holding in for far too long. A torrent of anger billowed from my lips like a cloud of poisonous ash as Eric stared back at me, bewildered.

"You want to take her away from me now? It's *easy* now. Now you get to go and have your fun pizza and movie dates. But where were you when she had strep throat for a year straight? When she had to get her tonsils removed? Her first day of school? Where were you when I had to do *everything*?"

I pressed a hand to my mouth to stop myself from saying more. Angry tears rimmed my eyes as I held my breath and tried to regain my composure. I exhaled, my head pounding as I realized Star was probably craning her neck to hear everything we said. *Fuck. I'm screwing things up again.*

I looked across the table where Eric sat quietly with his hands folded on the table, his eyes lowered. Guilt crept into my chest and sucked out the last bit of my energy.

"Sorry. I've been holding that in for a long time."

"It's okay. I deserve it." Eric unfolded his hands and

placed his palms flat on the table. "I wish I could go back and change things. Change who I was and what I did."

"Me too." I wiped my eyes. "I'm trying to let go, I really am. Please be patient with me. This is really hard."

"I know you don't want to take advice from me, but counseling really helps," he said softly. "It helped me, anyway. It's just good to have someone to talk to."

I nodded. "I know. I'm looking into some places, but a lot of them are expensive. The ones I can afford have a wait list."

Eric nodded. "Anyway, I won't take up your time. I'm moving into the apartment this weekend. It's just fifteen minutes away, right over the bridge."

"Okay."

"Veronica."

I met his gaze. It had been a long time since I heard him say my name. It was hard to hold onto my anger. He was still in there, the goofy kid I met on the first day of community college. Two weird loners with sad pasts who briefly found comfort in one another. So much of me still resented him, but I couldn't hate him.

"I'm sorry," he said. "I don't know if I ever really told you that, but I am."

"I know."

Eric stood up and brushed his hands on top of his jeans. "I'm gonna say bye to Star and head out."

I stood and waited as Eric said goodbye to our daughter. I followed him to the door and walked him out. The ghosts in my trees shivered against the night breeze. It was time to put my Halloween decorations away.

"I'll pick her up again next Friday if that's okay," Eric said.

"Of course it is." I laughed and wiped my face again. My eyes were still leaking. "Oh, God. Why is life so shitty?"

"I'm learning it doesn't have to be," he said. "I'm just so grateful for this second chance. I don't wanna screw it up." Eric let out a choked sort of sound as I embraced him in my driveway.

Sobs ripped through my body like crashing waves as we held onto each other and let go all at once. Over a decade had passed with so much anger, so much loneliness and sorrow. The canyon that divided us was wide, but for Star, I would work to build a bridge.

"We'll figure it out," I said. "We'll do better."

I pulled away, and Eric nodded, unable to look me in the eye. He wiped his face with the back of his sleeve and retrieved his car keys from his pocket.

"Thanks, Ronnie," he said with a sigh. "It feels good to be able to talk to you again."

I smiled and stood back as he got into his Jeep. I had to admit, he was right.

"Yeah. It's good to be able to talk to you, too."

I stood in my driveway and watched until Eric's headlights disappeared. I shoved my hands in my pockets, turned back toward the house, and nearly banged into the gauze ghost hanging from my tree. I let out a yelp and pushed the decoration out of my face. The white fabric tendrils danced on the wind and when they fell away, I glanced up at the house and gasped.

My grandmother hovered in the air, her slippered feet just grazing the roof. She stared down at me, her eyes laser-focused on mine, her bouffant of cottony hair whirling in the breeze. She spoke to me without moving her lips, her voice as clear as the last time we spoke.

Get out, she said. *Get out while you still can.*

Chapter Twenty

VERONICA

MADELINE MARQUETTE WAS NOT happy I sold her credenza. She didn't have to tell me. I just knew. From that day on, my grandmother showed herself to me in the most random and disturbing ways. Sometimes I would only catch her from the corner of my eye. Sometimes she would appear as a fully formed apparition in the empty space in my dining room where the credenza had been. Thankfully, she never appeared in front of Star. I felt her eyes at my back as I worked in my office. I sensed her presence with me as I bid on new items for my store at auction. I smelled her perfume in the car as I drove to the post office. My grandmother was everywhere and nowhere all at once.

Even though I sensed that my own grip on reality might be slipping, I wasn't too far gone. Not yet, anyway. Work was business as usual, things quieted down at home, and I was finally able to make a counseling appointment for Star through her school. She began meetings on Tuesdays and Thursdays, and a huge relief lifted off my shoulders. Even if we hadn't gone through a tough time, even if her father hadn't re-entered her life, it was good for her to have someone to talk to. Middle school was a tough time and I wished I'd been able to have someone to bounce my feelings off of instead of writing it all down in a flimsy Lisa Frank journal from the book fair.

I knew I still needed counseling, but asking for help and affording it was half the battle. Even if I could find a reasonably priced counselor for myself, what would I tell them? Where would I begin? Telling a mental health professional I was being haunted by my dead grandmother would only get Star taken away from me. Sure, I would have loved to unpack all of the trauma from my mother and absent father and from being abandoned after Star was born. I just didn't know where to begin, what to leave out, who to trust. I had hoped selling the credenza would reset things at home, but in some ways, it only made things worse.

"You got a package in the mail."

Star plunked a large manilla envelope on my desk one day in mid-November. I was still at my desk updating my online storefront when Star came home from school with the mail. The package was covered in stamps and labels that indicated it had passed through customs. The envelope was thick and heavy, and my best guess was that it held a book or magazine of some kind. The label was addressed to me in scrawling handwriting that I did not recognize.

"Huh, that's weird. I haven't ordered anything recently."

Star hovered over my shoulder as I broke the seal. She always liked watching me open packages ever since she was little, nosily wondering if the contents inside were for her. She was usually disappointed to find the packages didn't contain toys but antique jewelry or vintage articles I had won at auction.

The contents of this particular package were none of the above.

"What is it?" Star tapped her foot behind me, impatient.

I slid the contents out on my desk, even more puzzled than before. It was indeed a book, a very old one, packaged carefully in plastic and bubble wrap. I peeled away the protective layers to reveal a square leatherbound book the size and shape of an old-fashioned register. The front cover was well-worn and embossed with gold in the outline of a gnarled tree. I knew only little about antique books, but my guess was that this particular tome was at least a hundred years old, if not more.

"I think I need gloves before I examine this thing."

I reached into the bottom of my desk drawer and pulled out a pair of white cotton gloves.

"Why do you need to do that?"

"To protect the pages. Our hands have oil and other stuff that can ruin old paper." I slid the gloves on and cleared a space on my work table. "Star, can you turn on that overhead light?"

"Yeah."

I opened the cover of the book to the first page and was hit with a strange aroma. I wrinkled my nose and turned to Star.

"We better get masks on. Can you grab a couple for me from the bottom drawer? There's something funky in this book."

"Don't all books smell a little funky?" Star asked, reaching for the masks.

"Not like this."

Star affixed a mask on her face, and I put on mine before proceeding to flip pages again. The book contained hand-written pages and illustrations in an unfamiliar language. The dates I could make out, though, starting at the front with 1614. As I gently turned the pages, I came upon what looked like lists of names and locations. Copenhagen was among them.

"What is this?" Star asked.

"Not sure," I said. "The real question is, who sent this to us and why."

The years rolled by with every turn of the page, displaying more lists of names and dates and locations. Finally, when I reached the 1800s, I spied a name I'd seen before.

"Look. Here." I pointed with a gloved finger. "See that?"

"Peter Beck?"

I nodded. "Mhmm. Gran's maiden name was Beck. Maybe this is some kind of family tree or record."

"Wait, didn't Gran's family come from France?" Star asked. "This writing doesn't look French to me."

"Yeah, it was France, then Canada. She doesn't know much about her father's side, though. I've often thought about getting one of those genealogy tests to find out more about our family."

"So, do you think that whoever sent this to you is a distant relative?"

"Maybe."

I turned the page and was met with another family tree. *Andersen, Lars.* The records stopped in the mid-1960s. Then, I spotted a name that I definitely remembered. *Andersen, Raymond.*

"Wasn't that the name of the guy in your phone?" Star said. "The beheaded guy?"

Something heavy pressed at my back. The scent of my grandmother's White Diamonds perfume wafted through the paper mask over my face. I closed the book.

"Is there anything else in that envelope? A note or something?" I took off the mask, picked up the envelope, and shook it out. Nothing. "This is so bizarre."

"Maybe the post office can tell you where it came from?"

I glanced down at the return address. "Yeah, maybe. I think what I really need is a translator."

———

Finding someone local who could read and translate Dutch to English proved to be a challenge. Every Dutch translator in the state who I could find was over two hours away, in Orlando or Miami, and they weren't willing to travel. I had booths booked at the downtown market all weekend and wasn't willing to leave Star all alone, so traveling to see a translator wasn't possible either. Thankfully, living in the 21st century gave me an easier route: finding a translator online.

Carla was a Dutch woman living in Spain who agreed to create a voice recording for me of her reading the pages of the book out loud. I would send her photographs of the book and she would read them and send me a recording at the rate of $50 per hour. I couldn't afford to have her translate the entire book without dipping into our vacation savings fund, so I chose passages that seemed like they might be important. I would have to wait at least a week for her first translations to come through, but until then, I tried to do some digging on my own.

"Uncle Mike? Hey, it's me."

"Ronnie. How's everything going?" The sound of clanking metal in the background told me he was busy. I didn't have much time. *Best to keep this brief.*

"Uncle Mike, what do you know about Grandma's paternal side of the family?"

"The what?"

"The paternal side. Of Grandma's family. You know, the Becks."

"Oh. Not much. She had some cousins, I think. Up

in Lancaster. Apparently, her dad ran away from the family when he was a teenager."

"Lancaster. You mean, the Amish?"

"Yep. I guess he left the group in the 1920s or so? Grandpa Jacob didn't talk much about it when we visited him. He showed us how to work with wood though. He was an excellent craftsman."

"A craftsman, huh," I said. "What did he make?"

"Oh, furniture mostly."

I closed my eyes. Of course, he made furniture.

"I know this is going to sound weird, but did he ever talk about his religious beliefs or anything?"

"Ronnie, what's this all about?"

"I got a weird book in the mail," I said. "It looks like some kind of family tree. I don't know who sent it to me. Anyway, I know you're busy, but I just really need some answers."

Uncle Mike grunted in the receiver. "I honestly don't remember. Your great-grandpa Jacob was an old-school kinda guy. Even though he broke away from the Amish, he still believed in God and devils and all that. I never really listened, though."

"Okay, well, if you think of anything or remember anything, will you call me?"

"Yep. I sure will."

"Thanks, Uncle Mike."

"Okay, bye."

Click.

Great. My uncle probably thought I was just another crazy Marquette woman. I waited until Star was in bed before I pulled out the book again. I wished I knew who sent it and why. Maybe I really didn't want to know.

There was a time when I was younger when I thought I wanted to know about my family tree. *Was it third grade, maybe?* I never really gave much thought to the missing pieces of my family before then. I knew that other kids had fathers, but it didn't feel strange to me that I didn't have one. I asked about him that year, but Grandma Maddie only told me I didn't have one. Maybe I was the result of an affair. Maybe my real father was living the good life somewhere with the family he valued over me. By the time Star came along, I stopped giving him much thought at all. If my father wanted to be around, he would be.

I picked up my phone and scrolled through health-care providers again until my eyes grew tired. I wanted to at least give counseling a try, even if I had to withhold some of the more wild and unbelievable truths from my life. I was desperate to talk to someone, and outside of Star and Eric, I really didn't have anyone. I turned out the light and slipped into bed as I caught a pair of eyes watching me from the corner of my bedroom. My grandmother's scent filled the space, and I felt slightly more at ease. Less afraid. Less alone.

Chapter Twenty-One

VERONICA

THE WEEK of Thanksgiving snuck up on me like a snake in the grass. I think, in my own way, I was trying to forget about the holiday altogether. This would be my first Thanksgiving without my grandmother, after all. Every year, Star and I spent the holiday at Heron's Glen eating turkey and mashed potatoes with all of the other seniors. We would watch *A Miracle on 34th Street* and set up a little artificial Christmas tree for my grandmother on top of the credenza. This year, I would spend the holiday alone while Star visited Eric's family. The entire situation made me feel numb and hollow all at once.

I tried to distract myself with busy work like I always did. As Star got older and didn't need my constant attention, I adopted the habit of filling every hour of my day with chores or activities to keep from feeling lonely or anxious. I used DIY home improvement projects to fill the time gaps when she spent the night at a friend's or had some after-school activity. I could usually handle being away from her, but this was going to be a particularly hard week. I knew if I didn't keep my emotions in check, I was in for a tough time.

Eric picked up Star on Wednesday morning, promising to return her on Friday. I knew it was only two days more than their regular weekend visits, but I struggled just the same. *Star is nearly thirteen, and she's smart,* I chided myself. She had her phone and promised to check in often. Eric was no longer a danger, and she was comfortable with him. Still, a feeling of dread swam in the pit of my guts like a goldfish gaping in the air.

As soon as Eric's Jeep pulled out of the driveway, I grabbed my things and headed out to an estate sale Linda had tipped me off to. Normally, I'd bring Star with me to pre-Thanksgiving estate sales, and we would do our version of Black Friday shopping. This year, I decided to treat myself to a little self-care. I stopped by a local cafe for a frothy to-go cup of the sugariest coffee they had. I'd also budgeted a little extra to buy something that wasn't for my shop for a change. Retail therapy, my grandmother used to call it. This year, I would be filling the Star-shaped hole in my heart with sweet treats and a vintage purse.

The estate sale was about an hour out of town, deep in the heart of Central Florida. Here, the sprawling suburbs and strip malls gave way to endless miles of cow pastures, citrus orchards, and lonely farmhouses. My stomach was in knots as I drove past the scrub brush and slash pine landscape, but I remained hopeful for the day ahead. I sipped on my coffee as I watched the city give way to country roads, glad I decided not to torture myself during Star's absence. In fact, I could make these next few days alone a good thing after all. Practice for when Star is off at college someday. I could get my nails done or take a long stroll through the park. I would force myself to be okay with being all by myself.

I turned down a dirt road, my little sedan bumping along the way until I came upon a mailbox. I parked the car, lowered my sunglasses, and checked the address I had plugged into the GPS again. There were no other cars at the house, which was surprising, but what was even more surprising was the house itself. There were very few homes left standing this far south that predated the mid-1900s. Any century homes had long been demolished, turned into museums, or swept away by hurricanes. I thought that I knew every historical property within a fifty-mile radius of my home, but somehow, this one had escaped my research. I walked up to the Victorian-style home and marveled at the wraparound porch, gabled roof, and rounded tower. The powder blue siding and white trim could have used a fresh coat of paint, but otherwise, the estate looked worn but structurally sound from the outside anyway.

"Veronica, so glad you could make it."

Linda greeted me with a European-style double-cheeked kiss, her red Estee Lauder lipstick no doubt marking the side of my cheek.

I absent-mindedly wiped my face and glanced up at the entryway. The front double doors were gorgeous, inlaid with a rainbow of cut glass in the shape of a peacock.

"How did you snag this listing?" I asked, taking off my sunglasses. "This house is magnificent!"

"Isn't it amazing? It's going up for auction after I clear everything out," Linda said, giddy. "I would buy it myself, but Larry would *kill* me. I know it looks great, but this house has terrible bones. The owner hasn't made any updates since before Nixon was in office."

"Where is everyone else?" I asked, stepping over the threshold. "A house like this would surely have cars parked for a mile."

"I'm not opening the official estate sale until Friday." Linda winked. "I wanted you to get first pick."

"Thanks." I took a sip of my coffee and made a face. It was cold. "I'll just go take a look around then?"

"Yes, by all means. Be sure to check out the kitchen. I think I saw some beautiful La Creuset there."

I gripped my cup and walked slowly through the front parlor, taking in the dated decor. Much like my own house, this place, too, was a time capsule, though a far dustier one. The framed photographs on the wall were blanketed in dust, most of them black and white. Cobwebs shivered at the corners of the case bookshelf, stuffed to the brim with books dating back to the turn of the century. Heavy wooden Art Deco furniture finished in threadbare velvet and intricate tapestry outfitted the sitting area. There wasn't a single modern item in the front hall or the parlor to suggest that time had progressed past the 1960s.

"What do you know about the owners of this house?" I called out, making my way to the kitchen.

"Oh, not too much." Linda's voice echoed back. "Some kind of cow farmer, I think. Old money. The woman who owned the house was nearly a hundred!"

"Oh really? And she was still living here all by herself?" I walked into the kitchen and wrinkled my nose. There must have been a leaky pipe somewhere.

"No, she had been living in town. Assisted living," Linda said.

The back of my neck bristled.

"Heron's Glen?"

"Oh, I'm not sure."

I walked over to the farmhouse sink, grasped the edge of the counter, and stared out the window into the back-yard. An orchard of twisted, dried-up orange trees surrounded the property like a fence, palmetto bushes and brambles of beautyberry choking the pathway between them. It had been a long time since those branches bore any fruit. My breathing slowed as I gazed out the window, my vision blurring against the graying sky. Then, a flicker of white. A jolt of lightning in my brain. I blinked, and my grandmother appeared at the edge of the treeline.

Look.

She raised a spindly arm, the loose fabric of her dressing gown flowing as she pointed to a spot just above my head. I followed the trail of her finger to see a set of cased shelves built into the cabinets over the sink. My pulse quickened as I took in the contents of the shelves: a pair of porcelain lamb salt and pepper shakers, a coffee cup, and a book. Anxiety spiked my blood as I realized it wasn't just any book, but a very familiar one bound in green fabric book cloth. Another *Voorschrift*. My hand instinctively shot out to grab it. I stuck the book in my bag as footsteps fell down the hall.

"Everything okay?"

I sucked in a quick breath and turned to see Linda smiling at me expectantly.

"Yeah, I just…I think that my allergies are getting to me?" I forced a smile. "I'm sorry. Thank you for inviting me here early, but I think I need to go home."

"Oh, I have some Benadryl. I can—"

"That's so nice of you, but I think I just need to head home." I leaned in and gave Linda a hasty hug. "I'll see you next time, okay?"

"Are you sure you don't want to stay?" Linda asked. "You didn't even get to check out the master bedroom upstairs."

"No, I've gotta go. I'll call you!"

I walked out the door and back to my car as fast as my feet could carry me. I didn't dare look back at the house, but I could feel my grandmother's eyes on me all the same. I started my car, and panic seized my chest, squeezing the breath out of me. I opened my bag and took out the book, flipping through it just to make sure I wasn't crazy. This book wasn't the same as the one I tried to burn, but the contents were the same. Rust-colored stains splotched the pages of this book here and there, and the cover was even more worn. *How many of these fucking books are there?*

I started the car, and as I drove home, I saw a new email come in. *Carla.* I let out a sigh of relief and crossed my fingers, hoping that she would be able to shed some light on the other strange book in my possession.

To: Veronica@veronicasvintage
From: Carla_Bruner

Dear Miss. Marquette,

After careful consideration, I must cancel the terms of our contract. I am a Christian woman, and I do not feel comfortable translating the contents of the pages you have sent. Thank you for understanding.

Sincerely,
Carla Bruner

Didn't feel comfortable translating? What the hell did that mean?

I held up my phone to text a response, but that's when I noticed the time. It was after five, and the sun was low in the sky. *How long had I been in that house anyway?* I couldn't have been there for more than ten minutes, yet somehow, hours had passed. Time had gotten away from me before, but there was no way that I had been in the house for that long.

I tossed my phone into the passenger seat; I shouldn't be texting and driving anyway. I wouldn't let Star so much as touch her phone when the time comes for her to learn how to drive. Still, as I sped down country roads back toward town, I couldn't stop thinking about Carla's response. What was in that family tree book that was so bad she refused to read it? I caught the *Voorschrift* out of the corner of my eye and shivered.

By the time I pulled into my neighborhood, it was fully night, though a warm, sunny glow still hung on the horizon. Mariah Carey's voice cooed over the radio about how all she wanted for Christmas was me, followed by Black Friday doorbuster ads. A few of my neighbors had begun to decorate early, their homes and surrounding palm trees lit up with red and green bulbs. If Star were with me, if all of the other crap that was going on wasn't happening, I might have felt festive. Merry, even. Instead, as I neared my home, the pit of dread in my stomach opened and rose up into my throat in a hot, acidic wave.

The glow on the horizon hadn't been coming from the setting sun. It was coming from my house.

Chapter Twenty-Two

LARS, 1960

LARS ANDERSEN WAS a gifted craftsman when it came to making furniture, though he did not enjoy his trade. In fact, he didn't enjoy most types of labor. He accepted his laziness and felt no shame about it. If he had his way, he would spend every day with a drink in his hand and a lusty wench on his lap. But drink and tobacco didn't come free. So when the strange man came into his shop requesting a custom commission, offering more than a fair price, Lars simply couldn't say no.

Lars had taken a few strange custom jobs in his day, but nothing quite like what the man requested. Once, he had been asked to make a double high chair for a set of twin boys. Another time, he had been commissioned to make an oversized bed frame for the mayor, big enough to accompany both of his wives. For this particular piece, the man wanted a custom Danish-style cabinet crafted from the wood of an old tree…and insisted Lars be sworn to secrecy.

The stranger hauled the wood into the shop with the help of four men from town. It was a dark, hardy wood that was not easy to work with, but the stranger had promised ten times what Lars usually charged. Lars normally kiln-dried and cut his own lumber to make his signature sideboards. Why this stranger insisted he use such old wood was beyond his understanding, but he was getting paid, so what did he care? He wouldn't have to work for months if he didn't want to and could visit the beer hall every day. He also had an entire shipment of furniture ready to send to America, where his cousin would sell his handcrafted wares to wealthy housewives. For Lars, the future looked bright. All he had to do was finish the piece and collect his reward.

Lars spent over a week cutting, sanding, and nailing the pieces of the sideboard together. It was an easy enough job, except at night. He wanted to finish the piece quickly and often stayed late in his shop. But as the evening hours grew late, he swore he heard the wood whispering to him. One night, when the sideboard was complete and he'd drank far too many schnapps, he laid across its wooden top, pressing his chest and belly into the smooth finish. He pressed his ear to the wood and let the gentle thrum coming from within lull him to sleep. By and by, he became more fond of the cabinet than he would have liked to admit. There are times when the cabinet even made him feel aroused.

And so Lars decided he wanted to keep the cabinet for himself.

Once he stained and polished it, he lovingly packed it up in foam and shipped it to America with the other furniture. He included a note for his cousin, instructing him not to sell it. With the money earned from the commission, he could join his cousin in America and start a new life. He couldn't possibly let the stranger have the wonderful cabinet that he made. It was his now to protect and to love.

And so, with his cabinet safely packed away on a ship across the sea, Lars set to the task of making a second cabinet of walnut. He cut and sanded, hewed, and hammered, though the color wasn't quite right. He added an extra layer of dark varnish and hoped that the man wouldn't notice the difference.

It was a bitterly cold day in late autumn when the stranger came to collect his commission. He came with a team of men, dressed head-to-toe in black, wearing thick boots and leather gloves. Their faces were grave as they approached Lars in his shop.

"Where is the credenza?"

"Why, it's here," Lars said, offering his most reassuring smile. "This is my finest work yet, I have no doubt."

The stranger's scowl deepened as he turned to one of his men. The stranger nodded, and the man took off one of his gloves. He approached the cabinet and laid a hand on top. The stranger let out a low, snorting laugh through his nose.

"Where is the real cabinet, Mr. Andersen?"

Lars swallowed, his throat suddenly dry.

"I'm not sure what you mean…"

"There are consequences for your actions, Mr. Andersen."

The stranger motioned to the other men.

Lars tried to back up, but he wasn't fast enough.

They easily subdued him, each man taking an arm or a leg.

"Help!" Lars cried, though he knew no one around could hear him. "For God's sake, someone help me!"

"God cannot help you here." The stranger sniffed and unsheathed a large knife from his belt.

Lars let out a scream as his gaze fell on the knife handle, a sinister piece made of twisted horn.

"I can get it back for you, I swear!" Lars pleaded. "It will take some time, but I assure you…"

"But my men and I are thirsty now," the stranger said, his tongue clicking in a demeaning *tsk, tsk, tsk.* "You have delayed our plans, Mr. Anderson. So unfortunate."

"No! Please!"

The stranger grabbed a handful of Lars's hair and brought his blade to where his Adam's apple bobbed in terror. The knife sizzled as it sliced through his skin, and Lars let out one last gurgled gasp. The stranger lifted Lars's head to his open jaw as hot arcs of blood poured into his mouth. When he had his fill, the men each took turns drinking from the decapitated body until their dark cloaks were soaked with gore.

"What do we do now?" One of the men asked.

The stranger returned the blade to his sheath, his teeth pink as he smiled.

"Now, we go to America."

With that, the men left the workshop, leaving Lars's decapitated body in a heap on the ground.

From the shadows, a woman watched, silent and still as a mouse.

Chapter Twenty-Three

VERONICA

FLAMES REFLECTED against my driver's side window, licking my face with orange lashes. I sat staring for a moment, my brain unable or unwilling to believe the reality playing out before my eyes. My house was on fire. The roof was ablaze as black smoke billowed from my busted windows, the damage already far too advanced for anything inside to be saved. The silhouette of a lone figure sat on my front lawn staring at the inferno in a crisscross seated position, as though in meditation. I recognized her right away. I got out of my car and walked on weak legs toward my mother.

"I'm so sorry, baby, but I had to do it." My mother gazed up at me, her eyes shining. "It's okay, though. You're gonna be safe now."

"You burned down my house!" I fell to my knees, my palms hitting the grass as I bent over. A great wail like a siren exploded from my body as a pair of thin arms wrapped around my waist.

"They tried to get us, but I wouldn't let them," she said. "Mom always tried to protect us, but I didn't know it at the time. I'm gonna do whatever I can to protect you, too."

"You're insane!" I pushed her off me.

"I had to do it! You have to cleanse it with fire; that's what Alma said. She doesn't speak very good English, and she's so old, but she was right."

"What the fuck are you even talking about?"

"The credenza, baby. I had to do it. You'll understand someday."

"Mom. I sold the credenza! It's not even in the house!" The tears came again as I slumped back onto the ground. Everything I owned, my entire life, had gone up in flames. All of my stock for the shop. All of the Star's baby pictures and things. All of the years of hard work restoring my home. Gone. Nothing now but smoke and memories.

"You sold it to that man?" My mother jumped to her feet, her eyes wide. "When? When did you sell it to him?"

"I don't know," I said between sobs. "A few weeks ago."

Sirens blared in the distance.

"Come on. We've got to go check on Star." She grabbed my hand and began to pull at my arm.

I yanked free from her grip. "You stay away from my daughter!"

The wail of the firetruck was louder now. My mother

turned her head toward the direction of the sirens, her features distorted in the orange firelight.

"They're coming." She leaned over, grabbed the side of my face, and stared into my eyes. "Don't trust anyone."

Like a rabbit, she darted off into the night.

The sirens grew closer as I sat on my lawn and watched all of my dreams burn to ash.

———

"No one even told me she had been released."

An officer whose name I didn't care to remember stood next to me with his pen poised over his notebook as I stared at the smoldering remnants of my home. The smell was horrific and wet, the scent of charred electronics and incinerated memories hanging heavily in the air. The fire department managed to put out the fire before it spread to any of my neighbors' homes, thankfully, but by all accounts, my property was a total loss. I'd had some pretty low points in my life before, but now I was dangerously close to hitting rock bottom.

"Can you spell that last name for me again?"

"Marquette. M-A-R-Q-U-E-T-T-E."

"And you're certain it was your mother who intentionally set your house on fire?"

The officer looked at me with what I could only describe as disbelief. If I wasn't already emotionally drained, I would have fought back. Of course, I was certain. *But I'm just another crazy Marquette woman, right?* I pulled my phone from my purse and sighed.

"I have cameras. I'm sure there's some footage of her doing it. Here, I can show you—"

"That's not necessary at the moment, ma'am."

"Okay."

Before I slid my phone back into my purse, I noticed I had some missed calls. The latest one was from a name I hadn't heard from in a while. *Fernando.*

"We just have a few more questions, and you can be on your way…"

"Miss Marquette?"

I glanced up at the familiar voice.

Officer Kincaid walked over to me with worry in her eyes. "Glad to see you're alright."

"They didn't tell me my mother had been released," I said, nodding toward the burnt-out shell of my home. "I told you. She's crazy."

"We've got an APB out for her. We'll do our best to bring her back in. I'm so sorry about all this. Do you have somewhere to go?"

I pursed my lips and shook my head. "Not really."

Officer Kincaid reached into her pocket, pulled out a card, and handed it to me. "There's a women's shelter at this church. Good people. It's a safe place to land until you can get things sorted out."

"Thanks." I snorted and took the card from her. "I'll think about it."

"Hey! Let me through! I know the homeowner!"

I turned as yet another familiar voice cut through the

noise. Fernando stood behind the line of caution tape, arguing with police officers. I looked at Officer Kincaid and nodded. "Can you let him through?"

"I'll go see."

Ten minutes later, I was in Fernando's car, driving away from the scene of the crime. I didn't have the heart yet to call Star and tell her that our house had burned down and everything she owned along with it. All of my photo albums, my stock for the store, everything. Gone. Insurance would cover the losses, but some things simply couldn't be replaced.

"I was in the neighborhood, and I saw the flames and commotion from the main road," Fernando said. "When you didn't pick up my call, I decided to come and take a look for myself."

"Thank you." I sunk into the seat, staring out the window at the dark night sky. "What am I gonna tell Star?"

"That's tough. I don't know." Fernando took my hand in his and squeezed. "Where is Star anyway?"

"At her dad's for Thanksgiving. I'm actually glad she isn't here to see this. It will be traumatizing enough when she finds out."

"You wanna go somewhere and get something to eat?"

"Thanks. I'm kind of gross, though. I smell like a campfire, and my face is a mess," I said.

"How about a drive-through coffee or hot chocolate or something then?"

"Yeah. A hot chocolate would be nice." I squeezed

his hand back. "Thank you. I'm really glad you're here. I don't really have anyone to call."

"So what happened? Did you leave the stove on or something?"

"No. My, um…my mother burned my house down."

"What?"

"Yeah. I told you. She's nuts."

"Damn, Ronnie. That's… I don't even know what to say."

"It's okay. You don't have to say anything. Hell, I don't know what to say about it. I'm just grateful that you're here."

"I'm glad I came then." Fernando let go of my hand and pointed towards the coffee shop. "I'm gonna pull in here. You need to use the bathroom or anything?"

"Actually, yeah, I gotta pee. Thanks."

Fernando parked at the coffee shop and ordered a coffee, a hot chocolate, and a dozen donuts while I found the ladies' room. After I relieved myself, I tried to avoid my reflection in the mirror as I washed my hands. But I caught a glimpse anyway. My hair was a helmet of tangles, and my eyes were puffy and red. I was a mess. My hackles suddenly raised as I felt a presence at my back. In the mirror reflection, a wisp of cotton hair peeked out from behind my shoulder, my grandmother's breath humid in my ear.

Listen to your mother.

I spun around, but as usual, I wasn't fast enough. She was gone.

"Just tell me what I need to do!" I shouted, my voice shrill as it bounced off the tiled bathroom wall.

No answer.

I swung open the door and stormed out of the bathroom, my eyes brimming with tears. *How much could a person cry before their tear ducts dried up?*

Fernando was already waiting for me in the car with the donuts and drinks, Christmas music piping out of the speakers. I was still a mess, and it was late, but I knew I needed to call my daughter. I slid into the passenger seat as Fernando handed me my hot chocolate.

"Here," he said. "I was thinking, do you have a place to go tonight?"

I shook my head. "I hadn't thought of that yet. I need to call Star first and tell her what happened before she hears it second-hand from Kayla or someone else."

"Who's Kayla?"

"Neighborhood kid." I took a sip of hot chocolate. "I'll probably try to find a hotel or something. One of the officers gave me a card for some shelter, but I don't want to take up space there for someone who really needs it."

"You could always come stay at my place," Fernando said. "My mom is having everyone over for Thanksgiving. You could join us if you want. No pressure. Just as friends."

"Thanks. I might take you up on that. I need to talk to Star first." I reached down and grabbed my bag. "God, what am I going to tell her?"

"You can just tell her there was a fire. You don't have

to tell her everything," Fernando said. "Not yet, anyway."

"I don't like keeping things from her," I said, taking another sip of hot chocolate. "But in this case, I might just wait until after the holiday to give her the full details. I don't want to ruin her time with Eric and his family."

"That's a good point." Fernando turned up the music a little. "Man, I just love this time of year. Did you know they have a drive-thru Christmas light thingy down by the beach already?"

"No," I said. "They sure are bumping up the holiday a little more each year."

"You wanna go drive through it while you call around and look for a hotel?"

"Yeah. That would be nice."

I sipped my hot cocoa and listened to the soothing sounds of jingling bells and familiar Christmas tunes as Fernando drove us downtown. We reached a block of the city already ablaze with twinkling multicolor lights. The cup was warm in my hand and I felt safe and secure, relaxed for the first time in a while as I let someone else take the wheel for a change. I took another sip of my drink and blinked as the twinkling lights began to blur. A funny taste filled my mouth as my vision continued to blur. Before I could speak, I realized I couldn't hold onto my cup any longer.

And then everything went black.

And so it began.

Chapter Twenty-Four

ALMA, 1960

"They beheaded the alderman. They'll be coming for us next."

Alma pulled her shawl tighter around her shoulders as she entered her family home and closed the front door behind her. It had begun to snow as she ran from the shadows of the grisly scene. She had failed her mission, and the old mothers wouldn't be pleased. She was still learning the ways of her family line. Her inheritance. Her gift and her curse.

Her grandmother sat by the fire knitting as she always did on nights such as these; cold, dark, and bitter. Dangerous for even the common man, but more so for those who love and protect the light. She was the eldest of the old mothers in their part of the world. Despite her very old age and poor eyesight, she still made the most beautiful shawls and scarves in the village. She also still called the shots when it came to defending their people against the dark arts of The Divinity.

"Beheaded? Well, Lars was never a good man. Not an evil man, but certainly not good."

"Are you listening to me, Gran? They're going to come for us next!"

"No, they won't, child," she said. "There's nothing left for their kind here in the old world. That was the last tree in our lands. Can't you feel it?"

Alma closed her eyes and concentrated. Her gran was right. The usual threads of voices, the spirits of all the old mothers past, had gone silent. In her heart, she knew the old mothers had nothing left to protect. For as long as time, she and her people had protected the secrets that lay beneath the gnarled trees, the bodies of the most evil, ancient creatures that roamed the earth disguised as men. Creatures who consumed flesh in order to gain immortality. Their evil souls seeped out into the earth and remained trapped within those trees. It was the task of the old mothers to bury those creatures, protect the trees, and contain the curse. For millennia, the old mothers had been able to keep The Divinity at bay. But like all good things, that era of protection had come to an end.

"And what of the cursed wood? Did you destroy the cabinet?"

"No." Alma hung her head. "The alderman sent it to America."

"America?"

"Yes. Andersen wanted to keep the piece he made for himself. He made a duplicate and tried to trick them."

"Hmm." Her grandmother chuckled. "Why should I be surprised? The wood is very powerful and persuasive. If it wanted to go to America, it would surely find a way."

"We need to leave, Gran. You're not safe here."

"I know how to handle myself." Her grandmother thrust the end of her gilded knitting needle in the ear. The sharpened tip glinted in the light of the fire. "Remember?"

"What do we do then?"

"You must follow them." The older woman stood from her place by the fire. She grazed a paper-soft hand over the top of her granddaughter's and placed the gilded knitting needle in her palm. "Find the wood. Protect the wood. Find other mothers, if you can. We are stronger together."

"But I can't leave you," Alma said. "And besides, they're flesh eaters! I saw them drink the alderman's blood…"

"Which is why you must go," her grandmother said. "We cannot let The Divinity thrive and spread into the hearts of men. We cannot let them bring Him back again."

Chapter Twenty-Five

VERONICA

THE FIRST THING I noticed when I woke up was the smell.

My nostrils twitched as the stench of rotten wood, leaky pipes, and decay crept into my nostrils. It was dark, but the sun peeked over the horizon through the tattered curtains in front of me. My mouth tasted like shit, my arms were heavy, and my brain struggled to put together a coherent thought. I didn't know where I was or what had happened, but one thing was clear. I was tied to a chair, and I was properly fucked.

The events leading up to that moment began to crystallize and form into a picture as I struggled against my binds. I remembered my house consumed in flames and my mother, wild and incoherent, as she fled into the night. Fernando driving me to…where did he drive me to? A cold sensation seeped into my chest as I realized he was the last person I was with before everything went dark.

I wiggled my arms and legs, trying to break free, until it dawned on me that it was pointless. My wrists were already rubbing raw, and pins and needles shot up and down my arms from being bound behind my back. My ankles were also secured to the legs of the chair, making it impossible for me to stand. The more coherent I became, the more I began to panic.

"Hello?" I called out, my voice hoarse.

Soft sunbeams shot through the curtains, the rays of early morning light illuminating the dust motes in the air. I was able to see my surroundings a little bit better than before. The wooden floorboards were familiar, and as I glanced around the room, I realized where Fernando had brought me.

"She's awake."

A woman's voice floated through the room as the sound of footsteps approached behind me. A woman in nurse scrubs walked in front of me and took a penlight from her breast pocket. She shined it in my face, and I winced.

"Open your eyes. I need to make sure they're dilating properly."

"What the fuck is this?"

"You want to be untied?"

"Yeah. That would be great."

"Open your eyes, and I'll see what I can do."

I took in a deep breath and opened my eyes against the bright light. The woman shined her pen light into both of my pupils, clicked it off, and returned it to her pocket. Floaters danced before my eyes as I tried to place where I knew her from. As my vision cleared, I realized where I knew her from.

"You work at Heron's Bay."

"Not too smart, are you?" The nurse *tsked* and shook her head. "Well, you seem to have recovered just fine from the last dosage. I think it's okay to give you another one."

"No! Please don't!" I begged. "I want to talk to my daughter."

The woman pulled a syringe from her pocket. "Don't worry. You'll see her soon."

"What? No!" I struggled against my binds. I wanted to punch and kick and bite, but there was nothing I could do.

"There's no point in fighting it," she said. "It was always going to end this way."

Blood pumped faster through my veins as the woman advanced toward me, and my surroundings became clear. I knew exactly where I was. In fact, I had been there just the day before. Linda. The house in the countryside. The *Voorschrift*. None of it made sense but the dots were beginning to connect. I shifted my body weight in the chair and wriggled back and forth, but she was too fast. The sharp poke of a needle pierced through my flesh as she injected something into my arm.

"Everyone will be here soon," she said. "Then He will be here and we'll all be free."

A warm, honey-like sensation spread from my bicep,

down my fingertips, and into my chest. My eyelids grew heavy again as I tried in vain to keep them open. They fluttered in a slow blink as a dark shadow passed before the soft morning light and a hand caressed my cheek.

———

It was night when I came to again. My head was heavy, my thoughts even more clouded than before. Voices spoke in hushed whispers behind me as I struggled to lift my head and hear what they had to say.

"What do you mean they couldn't find her?"

"It's fine. We only need one of them."

"I told Linda this wouldn't work."

I had been moved to a different room and tied to a plush velvet chair. Someone had changed me out of the clothes I wore the day before and into a hospital gown, and a tube ran down my leg connected to a catheter bag. I didn't feel any pain, and though I could lift my head, anything else was impossible to move. As my vision cleared, I realized I was in the dining room adjacent to the kitchen. Someone had removed the table and chairs and replaced them with my grandmother's credenza.

"She's awake." The nurse from before walked into the dining room, this time dressed in jeans and a beaded fall-leaf cardigan. She looked like she could be someone's grandmother, so unassuming. She took the light pen from her pocket and flashed it in my eyes. "Pupils are dilating. Excellent."

"Water," I croaked.

"We'll get you fixed up soon, don't worry." The woman patted me on the head. "If you're good, you'll even get to wear something nice. How does that sound?"

"Fuck you." I coughed, my mouth a desert.

"I know. It's not nice to be in your situation. Patients don't always act like themselves when they're in pain. It's all going to be over soon, though. You'll see."

The woman disappeared back into the kitchen as I strained to listen to the hushed voices coming from the other room. I wiggled my toes and tried to think of how I was going to get out of my situation. It didn't look good, but I was willing to do whatever it took to get away. Before I could even try, someone entered the dining room.

"Hi, Ronnie."

Fernando stood before me dressed in a button-down shirt and jeans, a sad expression across his face. He propped one hand on his hips and scratched the back of his neck. "I bet you're just made of questions right now."

"No. Everything makes total sense." I coughed. "Seriously, Fernando. What the fuck?"

"I didn't want it to go this way. I tried to do it the easy way. We all did. You're stubborn, though. Never want any help."

"Fernando, please just let me go," I whispered, tears springing to my eyes. "I'll do anything, I swear."

"Too late now," he said.

The roar of a car engine and the squeal of brakes sounded behind me. Car doors slammed, and the front door opened, followed by heavy footfalls on wood floors.

Chills rolled down my body when I heard the voice of the man approaching. I knew, deep down, that I would never get away.

"How is she, Fernando?"

Dietzer entered the living room and faced me, though he didn't look quite like I remembered. His dark hair had grayed and his features were more weathered and sunken than before. He wore a dark cloak over a dark suit and struck a ghastly profile, like some fucked up version of the Phantom of the Opera.

"She's awake. And mad."

Dietzer kneeled in front of me, the scent of decaying flesh reeking from every pore in his skin. I flinched as he opened his mouth to speak, and a horrible, putrid aroma wafted toward me.

"Get away from me."

"Her mother is spirited, too."

He snapped his fingers at someone standing behind me and held out his hand. The nurse from before handed him the green clothbound book. "I had hoped that you would do all of this willingly. I know how important family is to you, after all."

My eyes widened as he opened to the back of the book. He turned it to face me, but I couldn't bring myself to look at the gruesome scenes on the page.

"We are offering you an eternity of youth and success. Of course, these things come with a price, but doesn't everything?" Dietzer tapped the pages of the book. "You will read this and help us to perform the ceremony. Then all will be revealed."

"The hell I will."

"Hell has nothing to do with this. I suppose you need some more persuasion, huh?" Dietzer snapped his fingers again, and the nurse left the room. "We wanted my granddaughter to be here, but we could not find her. We were able to find someone else, though."

The nurse returned to the dining room, pushing a wheelchair. Seated in the chair, either dead or unconscious, was my mother.

"I don't understand," I said, my voice escalating into a shout. "Tell me what's going on!"

"Today in America is Thanksgiving," Dietzer said. "I will finally get to dine with my daughter."

"Who is your daughter?" My throat closed, and a tear trailed down my cheek.

I didn't have to ask. I already knew.

Dietzer smiled, brushed the tear from my cheek with his rotting finger, and stuck it in his mouth.

"Why, you are, of course."

Chapter Twenty-Six

VERONICA

MORE THAN A DOZEN people filled the room as I tried to comprehend the horrific event unfolding in front of my eyes. Everyone was dressed in festive fall wear and appeared at first to be elderly, but upon closer inspection, I wasn't so sure. Linda walked into the room dressed in a burnt orange pantsuit, a tattered copy of the *Voorschrift* in her hand. Like Dietzer, she seemed to have aged decades in the last twenty-four hours. I also recognized a much older, tired-looking version of Officer Kincaid. I didn't want any part of whatever was going on, but by all appearances, I wasn't going to have a choice in the matter.

"Mom," I said, my voice shaking. "Mom. Wake up!"

"She'll be asleep for a while yet," Dietzer said. "I brought her here as a sort of insurance policy. As I said before, I was hoping you would join us willingly, but I understand this sort of thing can be difficult to stomach. Either way, we need you to read for us."

"And if I don't?"

Dietzer nodded to a muscular, broad-shouldered man with a weathered face wearing a cream-colored button down and brown tie with matching polyester pants. The man opened the bottom drawer of the credenza and pulled out the horn-handled knife. I was so happy to have the credenza out of my hair that I had forgotten all about the knife. My pulse picked up speed as the man brought the blade to my sleeping mother's neck.

"Okay, I get the point," I said. "Why don't one of you just read it?"

Dietzer nodded to the man, and he took the blade from my mother's neck. "The incantation must be read by one of my daughters, or else we cannot begin the feast."

"What happens when I read it?"

"I know our customs must be strange to you," he said. "We've been doing this for a long time, though. Please just, as they say, *trust the process*."

"No. I want to know what is going to happen."

Dietzer sighed. "Well, if you really must know. First, we needed you to release the altar of your own volition. Thank you for that, by the way. Your grandmother and the Old Mother before you weren't so cooperative."

I closed my eyes. *Mom told me not to sell it. I should have listened to her.* "This is all my fault."

"No! This is a good thing," Dietzer said. "We can finally break the cycle together and become a family."

"You and I will never be family."

Dietzer nodded his head in my mother's direction. "If you don't do as we say, we will kill your mother. Then you. And thirty years from now, your daughter will be sitting right where you are with a daughter of her own. A daughter that I placed in her belly."

Bile rose to my throat. The idea of that ghoul touching Star made me want to burn everything down. Something snapped in my brain then, and pins and needles ran through my arms and legs. I could move them again, but just barely. I needed to bide my time.

"Fernando. You're really going to let him do this?"

"You don't understand. There's so much more than you know." Fernando unbuttoned his shirt and tossed it to the floor. "It's time, Ronnie. Please. Do this for me."

I wiggled my big toe inside my shoe. The ability to move my limbs was returning, painfully but slowly. *Bad guys like to monologue, right?* I needed to get them talking until I could move again.

"Maybe if you explained a little bit of what's going on here to me, then I would be more willing to go along with it."

Fernando exchanged a worried glance with Dietzer as he began to undo the belt on his pants. "How much should she know?"

"I'm surprised she hasn't figured it out by now." Dietzer kneeled so we were at eye level. The smell emanating from his flesh was so repulsive, I could taste it on my tongue. "This is only one of many cycles, my dear.

I have been harnessing the power of the sacred tree for longer than recorded history."

"And what power is that?"

"Rejuvenation, my dear." He traced a hand along his decaying jawline. "It's quite a tiresome process since I cannot touch the wood myself. The old mothers placed a charm on it long ago that I simply cannot break. However, if one of the mothers—like yourself—would release the tree to me freely, then I am able to perform my incantation."

I flexed my toes as the pins and needles sensation in my legs subsided. I swallowed as my gaze turned to Fernando. That snake. He was my friend. I trusted him. Had he been waiting in the wings for over a decade for this moment? Watching my grandmother, pretending to be my friend?

"Did my grandmother know?"

Dietzer shrugged. "I suspect Madeline knew enough not to give me what I wanted. She resisted the powers within and suppressed them in your mother. So long as she was alive, my people and I were forced to wait. But now we can complete the cycle. You can either join us or perish. The choice is up to you."

I glanced at my unconscious mother again. I had to get out of there and bring her with me. My grandmother refused to believe the truth, and I just followed along. We would all continue to suffer because of it. I was afraid to ask what would come next.

"I'm not going to do anything until you tell me exactly what will happen."

Dietzer sighed. "I think it will be best if we just show you."

Fernando dropped his pants to the floor and slid out of his boxers. He looked slightly afraid, and for a moment, I felt sorry for him. I averted my eyes, wincing at his naked form. From the corner of my eye, I saw him lie down on top of the credenza, face up. Linda passed the horn-handled knife to Dietzer as the group of people gathered around him. My pulse sped up as I realized what was about to happen. Each of the members of the group had a tattered copy of the *Voorschrift* in their hands. They began to recite a passage in unison. I forced myself to look as Dietzer stood over him. Even though Fernando had betrayed me, I couldn't stand to sit back and allow what would happen next.

"No! Please don't!"

"This must happen," he said. "For all of us, and for our God."

Dietzer raised the horn-handled knife high in the air and plunged it into the center of Fernando's exposed, soft belly.

Chapter Twenty-Seven

VERONICA

Fernando let out an unearthly scream as Dietzer sliced his torso open from his sternum to his pubic area. Blood and intestines poured from the opening in his body, flooding over the facade of the credenza in a gruesome waterfall. Fernando continued to scream as Dietzer gave the knife to Linda and plunged a hand deep inside his gut. He fished around nearly up to his elbows as though he were looking for something. After what felt like a torturous eternity, he finally pulled out a small, gore-covered bundle from deep inside Fernando's guts. At first, I thought he had harvested an internal organ, but as Dietzer turned to show me, I realized that the bundle had hair, hooves, and teeth.

"You may begin." Dietzer waved a bloody hand toward his congregation.

Linda took the blade to Fernando's throat as he let out one last gurgled scream. I watched helplessly as more blood gushed forth from his body, his arms and legs twitching. I wish I could have taken comfort as he finally closed his eyes and slipped away into oblivion, but the horrors continued to play out before me. Linda sawed and sliced until Fernando's head was removed entirely.

One by one, the members of Dietzer's fucked up supper club began to take their turn feasting on Fernando's body. The liver. The heart. A slice of his thigh. I gagged as Officer Kincaid used the knife to remove his genitalia. I couldn't watch what happened next.

"I know that this sort of thing isn't easy to stomach," Dietzer said. "The Old Mothers are a tender and sentimental bunch. If it helps, you should know Fernando did this willingly. When all is said and done, he'll return as a full-fledged member of the congregation."

Dietzer extended the bundle in my direction. "It is up to you now to complete the ritual. Read from the book. Awaken our God. You're a wonderful mother to Star. I know you'll do a fine job with this little miracle, too."

Dietzer placed the bundle in my lap. It was still warm, and Fernando's blood immediately began to spread across my thighs.

I shuddered. "No, I won't do it."

"But you must. One of the mothers must do it. If not you, then Star. Make a choice."

I glanced up at the horrible feast again. Linda had moved to the kitchen, where she was preparing Fernando's head in a roasting pan.

"Don't worry, my dear. Linda is an excellent cook. She'll prepare a meal for you that will be very palatable.

And once you recite the words and dine on flesh with us, you'll live forever, too."

———

Hours passed as the congregation consumed Fernando's beheaded body. I sat in my seat as the warm, wet creature rested in my lap, still deep in its slumber. Dietzer left me to consider my choices as he dined with his horrible congregation, tenderly sucking the meat from each of Fernando's fingers. With each bite, the group seemed to regain their youth, or at least, their younger form. The smell and sounds coming from the credenza were unlike anything I had ever experienced before.

The strength returned to my limbs as they feasted, so focused on consumption that they paid little attention to me. I was tied to the chair, but I knew, with some work, I could free myself. The hairy, hooved bundle in my lap was still and grotesque, something that I could never feel maternal warmth for. I could barely stand to look at it. But even if I were able to run, I would have to leave my mother, and that wasn't an option. She hadn't been a perfect mother, but she was the only one I had. She was fucked up because of whatever this was, not because she was inherently bad.

"Fire."

My ears perked up, and I looked at my mother. Her eyes were open, but she was still slumped on her side in the wheelchair. She blinked and motioned with her eyes toward her backside. Her lips parted, and I heard a barely audible whisper float over the wet slapping of lips and the chomping of bones.

"You have to cleanse it with fire."

I noticed a clear outline of a gas station lighter in the back pocket of her jeans. I glanced at my fully healed fingertip, remembering how the credenza had hurt me. How burning the wound seemed to be the only thing that stopped it from seeping. *Cleanse it with fire.* That was it. I needed to burn it all down. I didn't know how I was going to get free without them knowing or how I would be able to set a fire without an accelerant or without them extinguishing the flames. But I had to try.

"It's ready."

Linda emerged from the kitchen with a plate of food. Mashed potatoes, green bean casserole. There was even a dinner roll. In the center of it all was a single sliver of meat doused in brown gravy. By all appearances, it looked like a traditional American Thanksgiving meal, only I knew that wasn't turkey on the plate.

"Wonderful," Dietzer said, dabbing his lips with a napkin. His teeth were stained pink as he smiled at me, his facade now more youthful than ever. He held onto the horn-handled knife, the blade red with blood. In any other circumstance, one might have considered him handsome. I could see how my lonely, emotionally fragile mother might have been charmed by him in her youth, but those charms weren't going to work on me. In Dietzer, I only saw someone I despised.

"It's time now to complete the ritual."

I glanced over Linda's shoulder into the kitchen. A

roasting pan with Fernando's baked head in the center sat on the counter, the hair singed from his eyebrows and the top of his head. It looked very similar to the image in the *Voorschrift*, but it was even more gruesome in person. A slice of meat had been stripped from his cheek, no doubt the cutlet on the plate offered in front of me.

"We've found that it's more palatable for newcomers to take their communion in this way," Linda said, forking a slice of meat. "Open up."

My stomach lurched as Linda extended the fork toward my mouth. The thought of eating another human, especially one I had known, was too much to bear. I couldn't fall apart, though. Star needed her mother.

"No."

I locked onto Dietzer's gaze. A smile quirked at the corner of his mouth, and his eyes narrowed.

"You have no other choice."

"I've changed my mind," I said. "I'm tired of being poor, of worrying all the time. I want what you all have. But I want to do it the right way."

"And what way is that?"

"I don't need to be babied. I'll do it the right way. It doesn't need to be cooked."

Linda frowned and looked to Dietzer.

He picked at a string of meat in his teeth with the horn-handled knife and shrugged. "I suppose she really is my daughter after all. Untie her."

"But I worked so hard to cook this meal," Linda whined with a pout.

"Do as I say!" Dietzer's hand flew and struck the side of Linda's face.

The plate of food clattered to the floor, and the room went silent. Linda brought a hand to her cheek, lowered her eyes, and began to undo my ties. She lifted the bundle of gore from my lap and cradled the sleeping creature in her arms as Dietzer took my hand.

"We cannot deny our fate," Dietzer said. "We can only embrace it."

I stood on weakened legs as the blood rushed to my feet. I had to think fast.

"Wait." I glanced at my mother. "Let me turn her around. I don't want her to see me."

Dietzer waved the knife in my direction and nodded. "Go on. Be quick."

I walked toward my mother, her eyes open but limbs still slack as I rounded the back of the wheelchair. I grabbed the handles and turned her to face away from the credenza and what little was left of Fernando's corpse. I leaned in and wrapped my arms around her in what I was certain would be our last embrace and slid my hand along her back jeans pocket.

"I'm sorry I never believed you."

"Enough sentimentality," Dietzer said, waving the knife in warning. "Finish this. Now."

I straightened up and curled my fists into a ball as I walked toward the altar. The members of Dietzer's congregation stood back and stared at me as I approached the credenza, their mouths and hands stained red, the fronts of pleated polyester dresses and

Sunday best church suits dripping with gore. They each held a copy of the *Voorschrift* in their hands as though ready to recite a hymn. I reached the table and nearly gagged at the smell of Fernando's bowels. I clenched my jaw and turned to face Dietzer, using every last bit of my strength to put on a good act.

"Where is my book?"

"Oh, right." Linda snapped to action and retrieved my handbag. She dug inside and brought out the book I had pocketed from that very house only a day before. "Don't worry so much about pronouncing the words right. It's more about intention than accuracy."

She opened the book to a chapter titled "Ceremonie" and placed it in my left hand.

"You must consume the flesh and then recite the words," Dietzer said. "And then our God shall be reborn, and you too shall be born anew."

Dietzer took the horn-handled knife and sliced off a bit of meat from the back of Fernando's thigh. He handed the strip of flesh to me. I placed the book on top of the credenza and took it with my left hand. It was only a small piece, but I knew that no amount of acting or mentally blocking anything out could make me swallow it. I needed to work fast. I locked my gaze with Dietzer and held the meat near my mouth. His eyes sparkled as he watched with genuine interest, a cruel smile set on his blood-stained lips.

"You'll promise that Star won't have anything to do with this if I comply?"

Dietzer nodded.

I palmed my mother's lighter in my right hand, my heart beating fast as I held his gaze. "And you'll let my mother go?"

Dietzer chuckled. "If that is her wish."

"Then there's only one thing left to do."

I kept my gaze trained on Dietzer and ran my thumb along the flint of the lighter. It turned with a click, and a single flame sparked to life. I lowered the lighter onto the pages of the *Voorschrift* as his eyes grew wide. The cursed pages bloomed into a fireball, illuminating the room with its warm orange blaze.

Chapter Twenty-Eight

VERONICA

Screams rippled through the air as the flames from the *Voorschrift* blossomed and spread along Fernando's eviscerated corpse. Just like in my backyard, the pages of the cursed cookbook seemed to be soaked with gasoline, causing arcs of fire to spit out in all directions. I jumped back this time, anticipating the fiery explosion as it pushed me to the ground. The top of the credenza lit up like a Christmas tree decorated with candles, and I knew my plan had worked.

What happened next, though, was something I never could have anticipated.

One by one, the members of the congregation burst into flames. Sparks shot out from the top of their heads, their eyes, and their fingertips until each and every person was consumed by fire. Officer Kincaid spun in circles and jumped through the window as if she were an extra in an action film. Linda ran to the kitchen sink and tried to turn on the faucet, but it was far too late. The flames from her hair licked up the kitchen window curtains as she slumped over the sink in a heap of charred, melted skin. Lighting the credenza on fire caused them to ignite, too.

I didn't wait around to see what would happen next. Fueled by adrenaline, I pushed myself off the ground and ran toward my mother's wheelchair. I grabbed the handles and pushed her toward the door, not wanting to look back at the horrible scene. After seeing my own home go up in flames, I knew I didn't have much longer to get out before we became part of the barbecue.

"Hang on, Mom. We're getting outta here."

I spotted the front door, and hope sprung in my heart. *We're going to make it!* Just a few more steps to freedom. But something snagged my hair and curled around it, yanking me down. I came crashing to the floor, the breath stolen from my lungs in a sharp, agonizing blow. A kaleidoscope of colors danced before my eyes as I struggled against the crushing sensation in my skull. I needed to get up. I needed to get out. I need to get back to Star.

"You little bitch!"

A white-hot jab of pain pierced my shoulder as I stared into the scorched face of the man I most despised. Dietzer hovered over me, his blackened lips pulled back into a hateful sneer, his red eyes bulging. His flesh-stripped hand firmly grasped the horn handle of the knife as the blade sunk deep into my left shoulder.

"After I eat your heart, I'll go find your little bitch

daughter." He laughed, spittle smattering my cheek. "I can't be stopped. This will never end."

Dietzer pulled the blade from my shoulder, and I gasped and sputtered as he swung the knife high over his head. This was it. I was going to die. I had failed everyone: Grandma Maddie, my mother. Now, I was going to fail Star, too.

I looked up at the ceiling, prepared to meet my death. And that's when I saw her floating on the ceiling, staring down at me, her gown flowing like an angel. My grandmother smiled and shook her head. A great glowing ball of light emanated from the center of her chest as she placed a hand over her heart.

It's not time yet.

The heart. That was it.

I couldn't give up yet. I had to try.

Dark smoke filled the air as Dietzer brought the blade down. I quickly rolled on my side, and the knife stuck into the floorboards. Then I sprang to my feet, sputtering as my lungs burned. He struggled to free the knife from the wooden floor, giving me a moment to consider my options. I was no fighter. I didn't have a plan, but I knew I wouldn't stop until one of us was dead.

"Hey, asshole."

Dietzer looked up at me, his charred features twisted with rage. I didn't give him time to react. With a swing of my leg, I planted my foot under his chin. The ball of my foot connected with his skull and sent him sailing backward as more dark smoke billowed to the ceiling. He landed on his back and I lunged for the knife. As I gripped the horn handle, a pleasant sort of electricity traveled through my palm and up my arm to dance up the back of my spine. *Pleasure. Power. Pain.* It was all mine, all at my fingertips. In an instant, I knew why Dietzer fought so hard to keep that power all to himself. I needed to make sure no one could ever harness it again.

"You're weak." He rose to his feet, his gaze set on the knife. "You have no friends. No family. All you have is what I have allowed you to have. You're an ungrateful daughter."

I smirked, a bitter laugh puffing from my lips as I gripped the knife handle tighter. There was a new look in his eyes that I had never seen before.

"If I'm so weak, then why do you look afraid?"

"Your mother is weak, too. It's nature's way," he said, edging closer. "How do you think I was able to have my way with her? She was begging for someone to show her an ounce of attention."

Whatever animosity remained in my heart for my mother vanished at that moment. All of the anger and hurt and decades of estrangement seemed so insignificant now. I let those feelings go and replaced them with an even more powerful emotion. Vengeance.

"It's not too late, daughter." Dietzer held his arms open wide and attempted a smile. Displaying his teeth only made him look more like a ghoul. "You feel the power, don't you? I can show you how to use it. It's not too late."

"No," I said. "It's not too late."

I pretended to accept his embrace, only to lunge

forward and sink the blade into his chest. His burnt breastbone caved easily, allowing me to stab him directly in the heart. He let out only a small, surprised whimper, followed by a gurgling sound like a clogged drain filled with gelatinous muck. His skin liquified and ran down his face like an oil slick, revealing the white of his skull. With a shudder, the rest of his body melted around the bone-handle knife.

"Veronica." My mother coughed and choked. We were running out of time.

The growing flames licked my back as I pulled out the blade and tossed it into the blaze. A large beam crashed into the credenza's skeleton, causing me to rush to my mother. I grabbed the handles of the wheelchair and pushed her toward the front door as another beam crashed behind me into the inferno.

The cool November air washed over me as I ran from the house, my lungs desperately drinking the fresh air. I pushed her out as far as I could manage before doubling over and hacking out gobs of black, thick phlegm. Finally, when my breathing had somewhat settled, I turned to look at my mother. She stared at the house, her eyes shining.

"Mom?"

She turned to face me, her eyes brimming with tears, either from crying or being exposed to smoke. She let out a sob and clutched her hands to her chest.

"I told you," she said. "That thing was cursed."

Chapter Twenty-Nine

VERONICA

It was a long walk along the country road to the nearest gas station. With no phone, no money, and no vehicle, we had no choice. We both agreed there was no point sticking around when firefighters and police eventually showed up. Explaining what happened to the authorities would be impossible, and as Officer Kincaid, Fernando, and Linda showed me, not everyone could be trusted.

"I'm sorry I never told you the truth about your father." My mother sat up straighter in her seat as I pushed the wheelchair past a stop sign. "Your Grandma Maddie never believed me. She wouldn't let me talk about it."

The fluorescent lights of a Racetrack gas station hummed in the distance as the color of the sky overhead lightened. Just a little bit further and we would be able to get help. I would be able to get home to Star.

"I know. I know," she said, looking up at me. "But I want to."

"I'm sorry," I said.

"You don't have to keep apologizing, kid," she said. "I should apologize to you. I burned down your house, and the damned cabinet wasn't even in it."

"Yeah. About that…"

"I'm sorry. Truly, I am. There's no excuse for it. It's just… I've spent my life screaming into the void with no one to believe me. I knew you'd be the same. I just wanted to make sure you were safe."

"How did you break out of jail?"

"Break out?" My mother scoffed. "I didn't break out. Someone drugged me up and dragged me here, probably that Kincaid lady."

"Right." I bit my lip and shook my head. "My whole life is a lie. Everyone I thought was a friend was just plotting against me."

"Not everyone." She turned back to look at me again. "You got the family tree, right?"

"The weird book in the mail?"

"Yeah, I had your great Aunt Alma send it to you. Nice lady, but her English isn't so good. Then again, neither is my Dutch."

Sirens suddenly broke through the quiet of early morning, and I gazed back at the horizon to see plumes of smoke still billowing from the house fire. Someone must have finally called it in.

"We need to get to that gas station and hide," I said. "So, I have a great Aunt Alma?"

She nodded. "On your paternal grandfather's side. There aren't many of us left. The Old Mothers. She was one of the voices I used to hear. The ones who tried to warn me."

"You tried to tell me. You tried to tell all of us. We never believed you."

"I don't blame you," Mom said, her hand swatting away the words as though they were flies. "Kids never listen to advice from their parents. They gotta hear it from someone else. That's why I was hoping Alma would get through to you, but I guess it was too late."

"So all that was real?"

"Unfortunately. That credenza was made out of the last of the Dead Wood. That's what the Old Mothers in Colorado think, anyway."

"There are more like…them? Like the old mothers?"

"Like *us*," she said. "You, me, and Star."

"I still don't understand."

"When one of the members of The Divinity is executed and buried, a gnarled tree grows from their grave. Their essence is captured and trapped within the wood. Then those weirdos turn the wood into a dining table or something and use it for their cannibalistic initiation ceremonies." My mother let out a chuckle. "See how crazy that sounds? I suppose I wouldn't have believed it if I hadn't seen it myself."

"Okay, so the credenza was made from some kind of evil wood?"

"Yup. The old mothers figured it all out a long time ago. They swore to watch over the trees and protect the wood from being harvested so this would never happen."

"Sounds like a shitty gig."

"That's our lot, though, isn't it?" Mom sighed. "Life is one big shitty gig. There are a few good benefits, though."

She turned up and faced me again, her eyes red and puffy. I realized then she had likely been crying since the moment we left the house.

I swallowed as my own tears threatened to spill. I needed to keep it together and get us to the gas station before the fire department drove by and caught sight of two crying women on the side of the road.

"We're going to go into that gas station and try to call Star," I said. "I'll see if Eric can get us a cab to…somewhere, I don't know."

"Come out to Colorado," my mother said. "It's nice there. You can meet some of the others."

"Not like I have a house to go back to," I said and let out a dark chuckle. "Colorado might be a nice change, though. I'll see what Star thinks."

"I would like that. A lot."

The teenager behind the counter at the Racetrack regarded us with wide eyes as I rolled my mother through the gas station's double doors. I was still barefoot, wearing a hospital gown, dirty and covered in blood, and I'm sure we both smelled like a campfire, but I didn't care. I went to the coolers and grabbed a large bottle of water before returning to the counter and the bewildered attendant.

"I need to use your phone, please."

"We're not supposed to let customers use the phone," he said, his gaze darting from my mother back to me.

"Does it look like I care about 'supposed to'?" I slammed my hand on the counter.

The boy jumped, startled by the noise. I felt bad, but only for a moment. He grabbed the black desktop phone and pushed it toward me. "Here."

"We're going to take this bottled water, too." I picked up the receiver and winked at him. "Thanks, kid."

I dialed Star's number, my heart in my throat as I waited for her to pick up. It only rang once, and I nearly burst at the sound of her voice.

"Hello?"

"Hey, babe. It's me."

"Mom!" Star squealed in my ears.

The dam broke, and tears ran down my face.

"Kayla said the house burned down! Are you okay? Where are you?"

"I'm okay. I need some help, though. Your grandma is with me, and we need a ride. Can you put your dad on the phone?"

"Yeah, hold on."

The sound of ruffling fabric filled the receiver and I let out a sob into the crook of my elbow. I sniffed and pulled it together as Eric's voice sounded in my ear.

"Veronica. What happened?"

"Um, it's kind of hard to explain." I glanced up at the ceiling. "My mother and I need a ride and somewhere to stay. Do you think we could come to your place?"

"Of course. I told you that you were welcome for Thanksgiving. We have a ton of leftovers."

"Good. I'm starving." I let out a half-crazed laugh. "Could you send a cab out to the Racetrack on State Road 17 in Arcadia? I'll pay you back."

"Yeah, I'll call right away." Eric paused. "Star said your house burned down."

"It did. It was an accident, though." I glanced at my mother. She sipped the water, a guilty expression on her face. "We'll get it all sorted out. I just need somewhere soft to land for now."

"Okay. Hang tight. Someone will be on the way."

"Thank you," I said. "I owe you one."

"No, you don't. Just get here safe."

"Thanks, Eric."

"See you soon."

I hung up the phone and pushed it back toward the bewildered cashier. My stomach growled, and I realized it must have been over a day since I last ate anything. I grabbed a couple of protein bars from in front of the register and waved them at the kid.

"I'm taking these, too."

"Okay."

"We're gonna leave now. I'll send some cash for these. Promise."

"Sure, whatever."

"You're scaring the kid to death," my mom said. "Let's get out of here."

"Right."

I pushed my mother back out into the early morning light as a half-dozen police vehicles whizzed past with sirens blaring, followed by a fire truck, all heading toward the billowing smoke. I shielded my eyes, and relief flooded over me as a telltale yellow cab rolled into the gas station parking lot behind them.

"Well, looks like Eric isn't so useless after all," my mother said. "There's hope for all of us, isn't there?"

"I guess so." I put the brake on the wheelchair and nodded toward the cab. "Be right back."

"Cab for Marquette?" The driver, an older man with a Latin accent, asked.

I nodded. "Yes. Are you able to drive us far out of town?"

"Far as you need to go," the driver said. "Whoever called me already prepaid."

"Thank you, Eric," I said under my breath and turned toward my mom.

I went to push her in the wheelchair, but she swatted me away again. "I think I can try to walk okay now."

"You're sure?" I offered her my hand, which she took, and helped her out of the chair.

She stood on shaky legs and wrapped her arms around me. "Thank you for finally believing me. For giving me a second chance."

I nodded and hugged her back. "Thank you for never giving up. You really did keep us safe."

"I know." She pulled away, smiled, and walked toward the cab.

I opened the door and helped her in as the sun climbed higher in the sky. She eased into her seat, and I followed, sliding into the other seat beside her. My body ached. My mind raced with all of the things I still had to do and all of the possible questions that would come. Where we would live. How I would piece my life back together. But I knew all of that would come in time. For now, I still had my daughter, myself, and now, my mother, too. I glanced over at my mother and wondered if I would ever see my grandmother's spirit again. Maybe I was finally going to be able to let her go, too.

My mother patted my hand as if she knew what I was thinking. As if she knew all along. "It's gonna be okay, kid," she said. "Now, let's go have a proper Thanksgiving with my granddaughter."

Epilogue

"Wʜᴀᴛ ᴅᴏ ᴡᴇ ʜᴀᴠᴇ ʜᴇʀᴇ?"

Detective Ryan Alderman snapped on a fresh pair of gloves and cocked his head, examining the charred ruins beneath his feet. The arson investigation for the house fire just off of US-17 had been taking longer than he expected, and he was already anxious to return home. Even though the house was supposed to be vacant, more than a dozen bodies had been recovered so far by the forensics team. The Department of Homeland Security had Alderman flown in specially to report back on this particular case, but between the briefing he got and the evidence on the scene, he was puzzled.

Very little had remained after the fire, which arson units believed was started with some kind of accelerant. However, as he toed the charcoal with the tip of his boot, something strange glinted in the afternoon sunlight. He bent over and brushed away the debris to reveal an unusual knife. The blade was long and sharp, and the handle was twisted like the horn of a goat. As he palmed the knife, his adrenal glands pumped, and the hair stood on the back of his neck.

Alderman looked around to see if anyone was watching. Most of the recovery crew had gone, and he was currently the only investigator on the scene. How could the other search party members have missed such an obvious piece of evidence was beyond him. It was almost as though the knife had been planted there. Waiting. For him.

Use it.

A voice whispered in his ear, snakelike and hideous. A warm sensation coated his brain like a tight-fitting cap, and his face went numb with pleasure.

It's yours now, the voice said. *Find the tree.*

"Hey, Alderman! Got your coffee!" Detective Jensen held up a styrofoam cup of coffee from the outskirts of the fire. She cocked her head to the side and gave him a funny look.

"I'll be right there!" Alderman forced a smile and waved back.

Jensen turned, and he dropped the smile.

The detective hitched up his pant leg and stashed the knife in his boot as black roots sprung through his veins, filling him with hate. The voice *was* right. The knife was *his* now.

And he definitely planned to find a way to use it.

Acknowledgments

This book is a Gothic love letter to my mother, Laura Owen, her mother, Jeanne McPhee, and my other grandmother, Grace Owen. Hopefully, the mid-century cabinet I inherited from Grandma Jeanne isn't really cursed.

This book (and all of my publications) wouldn't be possible without the love and support of my family and friends. Your support gives me the courage to keep going. Thanks, Mom and Dad, thank you Dave and my boys. Thank you, Teri and Jenna, Phoenix, Katie, Tammy, Nana, and everyone else who has helped me along the way. I love you.

Thank you to Paulette Kennedy and Catherine McCarthy for reading and blurbing advanced copies of this book. It's a real gift to be read by two authors I admire and look up to.

Thank you, Cassandra Wells, for providing inspiration for my main character. She's not you, but she's just as cool as you!

Thank you to my editor and publisher Cassandra Thompson for leaning into the pink side of Gothic horror. I'm so happy to know you and work with you!

And thank you, reader, for spending time with my words.

About the Author

Wendy Dalrymple loves to explore the beauty in horrific things. When she's not writing femme-focused #pinkhorror, you can find her hiking with her family, painting (bad) wall art, and trying to grow as many pineapples as possible. Find her at wendydalrymple.com

Thank You for Reading

Thank you for reading *Credenza*. We deeply appreciate our readers, and are grateful for everyone who takes the time to leave us a review. If you're interested, please visit our website to find review links. Your reviews help small presses and indie authors thrive, and we appreciate your support.

More Feminist Horror by Quill & Crow

The Bone Drenched Woods

The Secrets of Blackthorn House

Ending in Ashes